Will Northaway
and the Fight for Freedom

YOUNG AMERICAN PATRIOTS
BOOK TWO

Will Northaway & The Fight for Freedom

Susan Olasky

CROSSWAY BOOKS

A DIVISION OF
GOOD NEWS PUBLISHERS
WHEATON, ILLINOIS

Will Northaway and the Fight for Freedom

Copyright © 2004 by Susan Olasky

Published by Crossway Books
        a division of Good News Publishers
        1300 Crescent Street
        Wheaton, Illinois 60187

Cover design: David LaPlaca

Cover illustration: Thomas LaPadula

First printing 2004

Printed in the United States of America

Library of Congress Cataloging-in-Publication Data
Olasky, Susan,
   Will Northaway and the fight for freedom / Susan Olasky.
      p. cm. (Young American patriots ; bk. 2)
   As an apprentice to Mr. Spelman, the printer, Will begins his new life in Boston, where he experiences the violence aroused by the bitterness between the colonies and England.
   ISBN 1-58134-476-7 (TPB)
   1. United States—History—Colonial period, ca. 1600-1775—Juvenile fiction. [1. United States—History—Colonial period, ca. 1600-1775—Fiction. 2. Apprentices—Fiction. 3. Conduct of life—Fiction.] I. Title.
PZ7.O425Wg   2004
[Fic]—dc22   2003026752

CH		14	13	12	11	10	09	08	07	06	05	04
15	14	13	12	11	10	9	8	7	6	5	4	3	2	1

ONE

"Will Northaway!"

Will looked up from the table where he'd been peering at a frame of type. His back and neck ached from his cramped position, and he looked wistfully out the window where several boys were chasing pigs down the street.

"Will! Are you listening to me?"

"Sir?" he said to his master, who was glaring at him from across the room.

"This is the third time I've caught the same mistake on this broadside. Where is your head today? I'd take you out and whip you if I thought it would cure you of your lazy ways."

Will clenched a fist under the table. He'd been at the print shop since early morning, an hour at least before his master, Mr. Spelman, had come. He'd been hunched over his present task for more than two hours, staring at the little metal pieces of type until the letters swam before his eyes. He'd be blind before he was twenty at this rate. But he didn't speak his thoughts.

"Sorry," he muttered. "I'll do better. It's this heat."

"I don't want any excuses. I've heard too much blamed on this blasted heat—and your carelessness won't be put on that account."

For days Boston had been suffering under an August heat wave that caused short tempers across the city. People were angry and rude with each other in the streets and shops. As an apprentice, Will was often on the receiving end of his master's ill temper. After more than a year in his care, he'd learned to accept it. Sometimes at night he imagined how it would be when he had his own apprentice to boss around.

Just then the door opened, and a friend of the master's came in. The two men huddled together, speaking so softly that the boy couldn't hear them. Then his master took off his apron and hung it on one of the iron hooks.

"I'm going to close up early," he said. "After you clean up, run these handbills over to Jenkins's place on your way home. And mind you, I will have your hide if anything happens to them between here and there. Money is in short supply, and I can't afford the extra expense of any foolishness."

Will watched his master's back disappear down the street. Most likely they were off to the tavern where his master spent most of every evening. It's not that he drank that much—a glass or two of cider perhaps—but the tavern was the place people came to hear the news and talk about matters of concern. For the past several months no one talked about anything but the Stamp Tax.

Will swept the shop and left his own apron hanging next to his master's. Then he carefully placed the printed handbills in his leather satchel, picked up his cap, latched the door, and headed down the street. There was still another hour of daylight. Will rushed across town, darting in and out of alleys and across yards on his way to the hooper's shop.

The air had that still feeling that often comes before a storm, but unfortunately the rain never seemed to come. Gardens were wilted, and the ground was hard beneath the boy's feet. He wiped sweat from his brow.

Jenkins was locking up when Will arrived. "Mr. Jenkins," the boy cried. "Don't lock up. I've got the handbills from Mr. Spelman."

"You caught me just in time, Will. I'm off to the Liberty Tree." The hooper unlocked his door and pushed it open. Will followed him inside, breathing in deeply the smell of wood and glue. The fat hooper's shirt was soaked with sweat. Will set the handbills on the table and waited, tapping his foot and trying not to glance at the clock while the hooper read the broadside over.

"They look fine. Tell your master he does the best printing in Boston—and he makes his customers pay dearly for the service." The hooper laughed at his own joke as he waddled out the door, pulling it shut behind him.

Together they turned and headed toward the Liberty Tree, an ancient elm that had become the town's main gathering spot.

"What are you doing at the tree?" Will asked.

"We are gathering to protest the king's taxes," the hooper said. He rubbed his hands together eagerly. "Surely your master will be there."

Will shook his head. "I doubt it. My master likes to talk in the taverns, but I don't think you'll ever see him at a demonstration."

"Ah, yes." Jenkins smiled. "He's a cautious man and doesn't want to do anything that might hurt his business. And I'm the opposite," he added with a rich, rolling laugh. "Put me where the action is, and I'm happy."

They reached a corner where their paths split. The hooper waved and continued on his way. Will watched him for a minute or two. Then he turned toward home. He hadn't gone more than a block when he stopped again. "Why shouldn't I go to the Liberty Tree?" he asked himself. "Master Spelman didn't say I shouldn't."

That was true, as far as it went. But Will knew that his master opposed Boston's many demonstrations. Too often they turned violent, as Will had learned a year before. But the boy chose not to think about that right then. Instead he crossed the street and began to jog toward the tree, hoping to get there before the action started.

His stomach growled, reminding him that he hadn't eaten since noon. He knew if he hurried back to Mrs. Simpson's rooming house, where he lived, he would find some food put aside for him. But it would be cold, and he'd have to eat alone anyway. So he continued on to the Liberty Tree.

By then the sun was well down, and the faint outline of the moon formed a crescent in the sky. Even if the boy had not known where the tree was located, he could have found it that night. From a distance he could hear the raised voices of a crowd and see the glow of a bonfire. He drew closer, attracted to it like a moth to the flame. He felt excitement flutter in his stomach.

As the darkness deepened, men threw more wood on the fire until it seemed a mountain of fire. The flames roared and snapped, throwing sparks into the air. Voices grew louder, the laughter more explosive. Will drew close enough to hear the speeches, but he remained on the edge of the crowd. He searched for his master and was glad he didn't see him. Then he searched for his friend Samuel.

Blinded by the flames, he turned away. That's when he spotted a dark figure hanging from a low branch of the massive elm. He squinted and cried aloud: It was a body hanging by a rope, its heavy head drooping forward as though the neck were broken.

"That tax collector, Oliver, had better heed this warning, or he'll be hanging from the tree," the man next to him said.

Will turned to look at the apron-clad craftsman beside

him. "You can't just hang people you don't like. Where's the sheriff?"

The man laughed. "P'raps you need glasses, lad. It isn't Oliver, but his effigy. Maybe next time it'll be his sorry neck in a noose."

The boy felt a moment of doubt. He wanted to believe the man, but the dark form swinging from the tree looked too real. As he pushed closer, though, he saw that the figure was not a human body but a dummy made of hay. It wore a sign that said "Oliver."

Will began to laugh from embarrassment and relief. Tears rolled down his cheeks. When he saw someone whack the dummy with a stick, he joined in, punching at it with his fists until his laughter died.

"Enough of that," a man yelled. "It's time to cut the scoundrel down."

Will turned to see Thomas Mackintosh, a cobbler, directing the crowd. He knew Mackintosh all too well. A year before, the Scotsman had incited a mob to riot, and a little boy had been killed. Will had vowed to have nothing more to do with the man. Seeing him here spelled trouble, and Will turned to go.

When the effigy was cut down, the crowd surged in one direction, carrying Will along with it. He found it easier to become part of the stream than to fight against it. Soon the crowd had carried the effigy into the heart of Boston, past the courthouse, and toward the wharf.

People whooped and hollered as they walked, yelling Oliver's name as an oath. Every time the crowd heard it, the yells and screams became louder.

Many of the men were stumbling drunk. Their voices were loud, their language rough, and their tempers hot. The boy slowed his pace, letting the mob push its way around

him. Some of the men, especially the sailors, looked dangerous. Will didn't want to be too close to them, for many carried knives, and they all knew how to use them.

The crowd had grown so large it moved like a vast ser-
pent, snaking through Boston's narrow streets before finally
reaching the dock on King Street. When the head stopped, the
tail continued to surge forward until people were crushed
together in front of a small building.

"There's the tax office," someone yelled.

"Destroy it," cried a voice.

From out of nowhere axes, clubs, and bricks appeared.
Men swung their weapons fiercely, bashing in windows,
pulling down shutters, breaking in the door. Boards wres-
tled from the ruins became weapons in their hands. As the
violence worsened, Will watched the tradesmen melt into
the night, leaving dockworkers to carry out the destruction.

Within minutes the tax collector's office was gone, but
still the crowd milled about, unsatisfied by its night's work
and clearly wanting to do more damage. Boards and bricks
and broken glass littered the ground. Will kept expecting to
hear a constable's shout. It never came.

The destruction had taken place so quickly that Will,
watching from across the street, had no time to act. When
it was over, he looked at the tightly shuttered houses nearby
and wondered if someone had seen him. Maybe someone
had slipped into the alley and even now was fetching the
authorities.

Suddenly the crowd re-formed and began moving
toward Fort Hill. Curiosity outweighed caution, and Will followed them up the hill until they reached a house.

"It's Oliver's house."

"Teach him a lesson."

The mob, much smaller now, attacked the house, beating on the doors and breaking windows. Glass exploded and tinkled to the street. A few bold men broke open the doors and poured into the house, smashing everything in their path. When they realized the crowd had not followed them, they backed out.

As if a signal had been given, the crowd scattered. Even the men who had gone inside slunk away as if embarrassed by their actions. Will stayed in the shadows, unable to pull himself away. Finally, after glancing over his shoulder and seeing no one, he crept up the walk to the broken front door and peered in. He caught sight of a woman huddled in the hallway, shielding a young child in her skirts. She lifted her tear-streaked face and stared at Will. Though he had not touched a brick or club, he felt as guilty as if he'd been Mackintosh.

He turned away from her stare and ran for the safety of the boardinghouse, hoping no one was following him. He felt sorry for her, but now he was scared. She could identify him, and even though he'd had nothing to do with destroying her house, he was the only one stupid enough to be seen.

When he reached the boardinghouse, he found that Mrs. Simpson had left a plate for him in the kitchen, but Will had no appetite.

TWO

Will was at the print shop early the next morning, not wanting to give his master any reason to question him about his whereabouts the night before. By the time the printer came in at 8:00, the boy had already swept the shop, started the fire, mixed the ink, and broken down several trays of type called galleys.

Will hoped the activity would help him forget the woman's tearful face. But nothing seemed to work. All during the night he'd dreamed of her and of getting caught. He feared that he might be hanging from a tree if the woman identified him to the sheriff.

When Mr. Spelman arrived, he was already in a foul mood. He buzzed around the little shop like a hornet in a glass. Will kept quiet and tried to stay out of his way, but it didn't take long before the printer directed his anger at his apprentice.

"Where's the galley for the Adams broadside?" he demanded.

"I broke it down this morning," Will said.

"Stupid boy. Worst mistake I ever made, taking you on. Did I tell you I was through with it?"

As Mr. Spelman paused to catch his breath, the boy squeaked out a timid, "Yes!"

Spelman's face reddened. His jaw clenched and unclenched. "When? When did I tell you to break it down?" he demanded. "I don't remember it, and I can't figure out why I'd say that when I'm not done with it." The printer stalked around the shop, grabbing type and slamming it into the frame in front of him.

"But, Master Spelman," Will protested, "you finished that job yesterday and had me deliver it. Then you told me to break down the galley."

"Show some respect!" Spelman's voice sputtered.

Will sighed, hoping he'd heard the worst of his master's anger when the printer asked, "Where were you last night?"

The apprentice took a deep breath as he turned his back to his master. He didn't intend to lie, and yet he didn't intend to tell the whole truth either. Instead of answering directly, he asked, "Did you hear about Mr. Oliver's house?"

"Of course I did."

"What will happen to the ones who did it?"

"Ought to be horsewhipped and put in stocks," his master replied sternly. "The worst of them should be hung."

Will's mouth felt dry. He knew he'd sidetracked his master's anger, but he didn't really want to hear his master talk about the mob. Will figured he could escape a whipping at his master's hands. He had a much greater worry of falling into the hands of the law.

"What happened to Mr. Oliver and his family?" His voice caught as he asked the question.

"Oliver's a coward," Spelman said scornfully. "I don't have much good to say about the Stamp Tax. It will hurt my business. But if Oliver was supposed to collect it for the king, he had a duty to stay on and finish the job. Instead he chose to hightail it to safety."

"Where'd he go?"

"To a British ship in the harbor."

"I guess he was worried about his family."

"Should have thought of that before he accepted the job.

Of course the constable wouldn't protect him—he's afraid of the mob as well. Boston is full of cowards and scoundrels, and it appears that only the scoundrels have courage. But I wager they'll leave the poor man and his family alone now, which is a good thing for his family, but a bad thing for Boston. Now that the mob has tasted success, it will be even bolder next time."

The printer's anger passed, and for the next several hours the two worked together in a friendly manner. Spelman whistled under his breath as he operated the heavy wooden press. Will hunched over a bucket full of alkali, scrubbing inky plates and rollers until they were clean and his fingers were black. He hung wet pages on the line, broke apart galleys, and sorted the small pieces of type into their proper cases. It was boring work, which the boy hated, but it had to be done. If he made a mistake, he'd hear about it the next time those pieces were needed.

Lunchtime came and went, and the two never left the shop. They ate cold meat pies and cheese and washed the food down with cider. Will stretched his arms and legs, trying to get the cramps out, before setting back to work. He owed his master six more years of labor—and on hot days that time seemed to stretch very long into the future. The boy was nearly fourteen. He wouldn't be free until he was twenty, and that was a long time to wait.

At six o'clock Master Spelman took off his apron and hung it on the hook. "I'm leaving early today. Make sure you lock up—and latch the shutters. I'm afraid more trouble is coming tonight."

Will nodded and watched his master stroll down the street. Though the printer looked at ease, Will could tell he was worried, and that could only mean trouble for the boy. He took special care cleaning up. As he worked, he kept staring at the windows, trying to imagine what it would be like if someone started throwing rocks and bricks through the glass. Suddenly every noise seemed too loud—the ticking of the clock, the buzzing of a fly against the window, the scampering of a mouse across the floor.

After Will latched the last shutter and locked the door, the sun was a red orb in the western sky. Overhead, gulls fluttered. The boy absentmindedly threw pebbles at them. They flapped noisily, thinking he was throwing bread or something, but when they realized he had no food, they flew away.

When Will reached the boardinghouse, he found Mrs. Simpson standing at the door, wringing her hands and wearing a worried frown as she stared down the street. Her face lit up when she caught sight of him, but when she realized he wasn't her son Samuel, the smile disappeared and was replaced once again by the frown.

"Have you seen Samuel today?"

"No, ma'am," Will said, taking off his cap. "I haven't seen him since yesterday morning. He was still out when I came home last night."

"That's right, he was," she repeated as her frown deepened. "I don't like him being out at all hours. Not with all this trouble on the streets. I fear he may be hurt."

Will thought her fears well placed. Samuel had been babied by his mother and was itching for excitement. Mackintosh was just the sort of man to attract a boy like him. Will kept his worries to himself, though, and tried to comfort her.

"I wouldn't worry about him. He's nearly grown. But if you'd like, I'll go look for him."

"Would you?" she asked, favoring the boy with a grateful smile. "I know you think I'm silly, fretting over a big boy like Samuel, but I can't help but worry."

Will nodded. He couldn't remember much about his mother, and the thought of one worrying about him seemed odd yet comforting.

"You'll eat before you go," she said, bustling about in the kitchen.

Never one to turn away food, Will nodded. Then looking down at his inky hands, he trudged outside to the well and scrubbed them until they were nearly raw.

Mrs. Simpson set a plate of chicken stew and a glass of milk on the table. Instead of sitting down, she stood near him, wringing her hands absentmindedly as she stared out the window. Will gulped down the hot stew, burning the roof of his mouth in his hurry. He drank down the milk, pushed his chair back, and cleared his throat.

"I'll be off now," he said, shoving his hat on his head. "Please don't worry. I'm sure he's fine."

"You be careful, Will," she urged.

"Yes, ma'am, I will," he answered.

As Will hurried down the street, he thought about Samuel, who'd been his friend for the past year. He was a year older than Will. Folks said Samuel looked like his father, but Will didn't know about that since Samuel's father had been drowned in a fishing accident years before. Samuel was taller and better built than Will, but Will was the leader. He always had been, perhaps because Will had raised himself on the streets of London and could fend for himself, while Samuel had always had someone to care for him.

Will feared for Samuel. His friend longed to go to sea, but his mother wouldn't hear of it. To satisfy his desire for excitement, he would beg Will to tell tales of his months at sea and his life in London. And still he wanted more. Will knew that Samuel was out looking for trouble and that Mackintosh would be glad to provide it.

The boy walked to the Liberty Tree, figuring it would be the natural gathering place for a crowd. Sure enough, one already stood around the tree, and at the head of it was the redheaded Mackintosh. Will hoped to catch a glimpse of Samuel's sandy head, but since nearly everyone was wearing a tri-corner hat, it was almost impossible to tell.

Many members of the crowd were already drunk. Their mood was festive, as though fired up by the victory of the night before. The target seemed to have switched from Oliver to Thomas Hutchinson—an important man who held two jobs in Massachusetts. Hutchinson was both lieutenant governor and chief justice of the colony. Although he came from an old Boston family and had never lived in England, the crowd was suspicious of him.

Will knew that Hutchinson had been accused of sending secret messages in favor of the Stamp Tax to the king. Charges had swirled through Boston, been printed in the newspapers, and talked about in the taverns. Men like Mackintosh claimed that Hutchinson had a secret deal with the king, that he intended to betray his fellow citizens, that he was greedy for power and money.

Will didn't know what was true. He knew the Stamp Tax meant trouble for printers and lawyers. They had to pay a tax on every paper or legal document; so of course they were against it. And since printers owned presses and could publish their complaints, everyone knew why the Stamp Tax was bad.

But Hutchinson's role in the whole matter was much less clear to most people, except for Mackintosh and his friends. They didn't need proof. Will heard angry muttering every time the lieutenant governor's name came up, and the boy feared for him.

Mackintosh didn't leave the crowd's mood to chance.

As the moon rose in the night sky, he climbed up on a barrel and began to shout charges against Hutchinson. It didn't take long before he had moved the mob to action. Men poured into the streets just as they had the night before. Will followed, still searching for Samuel. This time they stopped in front of a house that Will guessed belonged to the lieutenant governor.

Light squeezed through the latched shutters, which covered windows that normally would be open to let in the night air. Mackintosh approached the house and began to shout demands.

"Mr. Hutchinson, you are a man of honor. We all believe that. So as a man of honor, come out. Face your fellow citizens. Tell us the truth. We want to know if you sent secret letters to the king, letters favoring the Stamp Tax. If you did not, it will be a simple thing for you to come out and tell the truth."

That speech met only silence. The mob waited for a shutter to open or the door to spring wide, but nothing happened.

The crowd grew restless, and voices began chanting, "Come out, Mr. Hutchinson. Come out. Tell the truth."

Will looked around at the angry faces and the upraised arms. Across the crowd he caught sight of a familiar face. Samuel, surrounded by a group of shouting young men, had his arm in the air and his face twisted into an angry sneer. Will pushed through the crowd until he reached his friend's side. Samuel was yelling something as Will grabbed him by the arm.

"What're you doing?" Samuel screamed. "Leave me alone."

"Your mother sent me to find you." Will hoped the mention of his mother would bring the boy to his senses, but it just seemed to make him angry.

"Leave me alone," he yelled. "I'm not a baby, and I'm not going home."

"She's worried about you. Besides, what do you know about the Stamp Tax? Leave it to them. What does it matter to us? They'll throw you to the wolves if anything happens."

Samuel hesitated, and Will pushed his point home. "Remember last year? Mackintosh's cart killed that boy and he never spent a day in jail."

Just as Will thought he'd gotten through, Samuel shook him off.

"Not now," he insisted pigheadedly. "We need to make Hutchinson pay for betraying us to the king."

Will's temper flared. "You're a fool," he barked, pulling him roughly by the arm. "You don't know a thing about politics. Just because Mackintosh says something, you think it's true."

"You don't know either," Samuel replied, a stubborn look on his face.

"But I'm not out here risking arrest. I promise if there's trouble, Mackintosh will not be in jail. No, it will be you and your ignorant friends who will pay."

Samuel looked so childish that Will thought he was going to put his hands over his ears and refuse to listen. But by then the crowd had begun to leave. Mackintosh stared at the retreating figures and looked like he was about to throw a tantrum. That night he couldn't find anyone willing to attack Thomas Hutchinson's house. Attacking him would be like attacking the king himself.

When Samuel saw the crowd thinning and realized that Mackintosh was afraid to carry out his threats, he let Will draw him away. They walked in silence. Though the apprentice could think of a thousand things to say, he decided to keep quiet, waiting for Samuel to speak.

"I suppose you'll tell Ma where I was," he finally said, hands stuffed in his pockets.

"She just asked me to find you," Will murmured. "That's what I've done. You can tell her what you please."

Samuel gave Will a grateful look. Then he punched him on the shoulder. "I was so close to an adventure," he said.

"Some adventure. I'd call it a riot."

THREE

After the second Stamp Tax riot, Will's master did a strange thing: He left town for a week. He hung a sign in the window, closed the shop, and left for places unknown.

Will had never known his master to take a vacation. He never did anything except work and go to the tavern. He liked to say that if you weren't working, you weren't making money, and the printer liked to make money.

Mr. Spelman left too quickly to set work aside for the boy. His last words before leaving were, "Obey Mrs. Simpson and do whatever you can to be helpful."

Will watched his master head off to the livery where he rented a horse. He was barely out of sight when Samuel slapped him on the back. "Don't look so forlorn, Will. He's gone, and you are free for a week. What shall we do?"

Will hadn't given much thought to what he'd do. The boy didn't have many friends because his master didn't like him spending time with the other apprentices. He feared Will would pick up wrong ideas. But Spelman liked Samuel, of course, for Samuel was his nephew. Will and Samuel often spent time together. But Will never knew what Samuel did all day besides running errands for his mother, delivering clean laundry to her customers.

"I guess I'll help you do your chores," he said.

"That won't take long, and Ma will let us do what we want."

"Don't you help her?"

"Sure. I run errands, but she doesn't pay me much mind."

Will discovered that his friend didn't do much work. After laboring for Mr. Spelman, Will felt guilty about wasting so much time. He kept hearing his master's voice in his ear reminding him to be diligent. But Samuel didn't seem to have such worries. So the two boys did very little work amid all their play.

On the second day of the vacation Samuel decided they should build a fort. The boys left the rooming house early and reached the marsh as the sun rose. Ducks and geese flapped out of the reeds. Pelicans swooped low, and sea gulls circled overhead. Rotted trees leaned dangerously, their few branches still providing homes for birds.

The two boys circled around the swamp, avoiding the sticky mud and trying to stay on firm ground. The smell of rotting grass and trees was strong. Thick clouds of insects swarmed overhead. Dragonflies flitted over the mucky surface.

"What a miserable place this is," Will shouted to Samuel, who was trudging on ahead. "Let's go back."

"But you haven't seen my cave," Samuel answered. "It's a great place for a fort."

Will followed unwillingly, swatting at the mosquitoes and blinking his eyes against the gnats. They turned away from the swamp and into a thicket of trees. Ahead, Samuel stopped at the base of an overturned tree.

"What happened to it?"

"Lightning maybe. But see how a cave was formed under its roots. It's big enough here to light a fire."

Will wandered forward and found a big hole in the ground where the tree roots had been. "What'll we make the fort out of?"

Samuel's face came alight. "I've been gathering wood and other stuff for a long time. I've got it all planned. But first we need to find more rocks."

That was easier said than done, because rocks were in short supply near the swamp. In the woods they found plenty of rocks, but it took them hours to drag enough back to the cave. For two days they labored on the fort, and by the time they were finished, they had a small structure with a smoke hole in its roof.

The fort was dim inside, for there were no windows, though light seeped in through cracks between the boards. The roof was so low that Samuel could not quite sit upright, but Will, who was a bit shorter, felt quite at home. They formed a ring with rocks, laid a fire, and decided to dedicate the cave by having a frog roast.

"You catch them, and I'll cook 'em," Will offered. He was nervous about getting too close to the fens, for he feared being sucked into the swampy mud.

"Nope. We both have to catch the frogs, but be careful not to step in quicksand." Samuel grinned at his friend.

"I guess you'd better be careful, too. I'd probably just leave you here if you fell in."

"You wouldn't," Samuel said.

"Try me."

"Well then, I guess we'd better stay together. I know some good places to catch frogs, and they aren't in the fens at all."

Will was relieved but didn't show it. They made their way through the cattails and tall grasses that bordered the fens, being careful to stay on hard ground. Again the mosquitoes swarmed around their bare arms and necks. A bullfrog croaked nearby.

"How do you expect to catch anything if you make so

much noise?" Will whispered to Samuel, who was whistling at the top of his voice. Then he spotted an old bullfrog and lunged for it, grabbing it by its hind legs as it leapt into the water.

"Knock him on the head."

"You knock him on the head." Will thrust the frog at Samuel.

Samuel gave his friend a puzzled look and promptly hit the animal on the head with a rock, knocking the frog senseless before sticking it in his pocket.

The two boys worked that way for several hours. Will was quicker than Samuel; so he was a better frog catcher. The older boy's clumsy attempts ended up with lots of noise and splashing water, but no frogs. But Samuel was definitely the better frog killer.

By the end of the hunt, their pockets bulged with slimy critters. They placed their catch on a rock while preparing the fire. It took a while for Samuel to start it, but the dry wood soon blazed until the little fort filled with smoke, and the heat became unbearable. Will pushed open the door to let in air, and the fire burned hotter.

"I'm going outside until it dies down," he said, letting the door slam shut behind him. He watched the smoke drift up from the chimney. Meanwhile he found a couple of long sticks and rubbed them against a rock until they were sharp.

Samuel joined him outside, and together they prepared the frogs for cooking—cutting off their heads, gutting them, and pushing the pointed sticks through them.

The boys went back into the little fort and found that the fire had burned down. They held their frogs over the embers, listening to them sizzle and watching as dripping grease caused the flames to flare up. They figured they were done when the frogs were black. Neither boy wanted to eat first. Finally Will nibbled timidly at a leg. The first bite tasted like ash, but every bite afterwards was delicious. Soon they had cooked and eaten all the frogs, leaving behind a small pile of bones. Then they set off for home.

The next day it rained. After helping with chores, Samuel and Will headed off to the Cromwell, one of the busiest taverns in Boston. Behind its white clapboard walls the Sons of Liberty—men like Sam Adams and Doc Warren— were said to plot treason against the king.

Last year Mr. Spelman had been a frequent visitor to the Cromwell, but he had become more quarrelsome as the year passed. He no longer enjoyed endlessly debating with Sam Adams about the virtue of liberty and self-government. He worried that his press would be shut down, and then his small income would shrink to almost nothing. For that reason, Will had not been in the tavern since winter; so he was surprised that the men inside knew Samuel.

Five or six men huddled at a table in the corner. Will recognized them, but he was shy around such famous people. Samuel, however, swaggered over to their table.

"Young Samuel," Sam Adams greeted him, clapping him on the back. "We haven't seen you for a while. How is your dear mother?"

"She's fine," he said, his chest swelling at the attention.

"Who's your friend?" Adams asked, looking at Will. The boy took off his hat, and Adams smiled when he saw who it was. "Will Northaway, I haven't seen you or your master for some time. He's too busy earning money to care about the state of liberty."

Will returned his smile with a weak grin, feeling disloyal listening to talk about his master that way.

Sam Adams rescued him by turning his attention back to Samuel. "There's a meeting tonight under the Liberty Tree.

We must challenge the citizens of Boston to protest this unjust tax. You boys should come."

"Will you be speaking?" Samuel asked.

"I may make a short address, and there will be other speeches. We must continue to fan the flames of liberty."

Will thought about these men comfortably seated in the tavern and compared them with the crowd outside Oliver's house. Again he saw the face of the woman hiding her child. "Don't you think Mackintosh has done enough damage?" Will asked Sam Adams. "Won't you be starting another riot?"

"I won't apologize for Mackintosh," Adams replied. "He takes our cries for relief and uses them for his own purposes. We've not called for mob action, and we've condemned the violence. But when there is grave injustice, it makes things easier for evil men to excuse their actions."

Will decided to be bold. "You speak about freedom," he said. "Boston needs the king's protection. The colonies are too weak. They need a strong friend like England to protect them from France." Will had heard his master say such things many times.

"Really?" Sam Adams looked at Will with interest, a smile on his face. "Is that your own idea? Or something you've been hearing around town."

The boy blushed. "My master says that it's folly to think about independence from England. He says we should find ways to get along with the king. If we are reasonable, then surely Parliament will be reasonable."

"Now we know why Master Spelman is spending so little time at the Cromwell. He's become a Tory. He didn't talk like that last year." When Will tried to interrupt, Sam Adams brushed him off. "Yes, he's a good man, but he's shortsighted, I think. Can't see much beyond his ledger."

Will didn't know how to answer. He turned to Samuel, who glared at him. "Let's go, Will," he said, pulling him by the shirt. Samuel dragged Will out of the inn and would have shoved him into the street if Will hadn't tripped.

"Why did you have to talk like that?" the older boy demanded when they were outside. "You purposely tried to embarrass me in front of them."

"I did not," Will denied. "He didn't seem to take my words amiss, except at the end. And I'm sure he's heard worse. Besides, how do you know he's right? I lived in London. I know how powerful the redcoats are. Boston is nothing but a puny town compared to London."

Since Samuel had never been outside Boston, he couldn't answer. He turned and stormed down the street, leaving Will to scurry after him.

FOUR

Will Northaway had been orphaned at an early age; so he never knew when exactly he was born. By the time he was old enough to care, his mother was dead, and his father had disappeared. Last year when he'd found his father after many years, the old man didn't even know he had a son. Will still blamed his father for a little boy's death the year before. Several months later his father, on his deathbed, had begged Will's forgiveness. The scene was still a bitter memory, though not as painful as it once had been.

Since the boy didn't have a proper birthday, he'd taken to celebrating it on August 26. There was no reason for that particular day; he'd just started doing it. It made him feel better knowing there was a day he could claim as his birthday.

Each year on that day he'd wake up and say, "Will, you're nine now." Or ten, or whatever. But this year he had hopes that it would be different. He was turning fourteen and finally had a family of sorts. He told Samuel his birthday was coming, and Samuel told his mother. When the boy woke up on the morning of August 26, a big plum cake awaited him.

"It's awfully sweet, son," Mrs. Simpson warned. "But Samuel said you'd never had a birthday cake before, and I thought you might like to have it for breakfast."

Will grinned as she sliced into the moist cake and laid a piece on his plate. It was at least three inches thick and full of dark pieces of plum. He made himself wait before tasting it, picking it up and enjoying the rich, spicy fragrance. He chewed each bite slowly, trying to make it last as long as possible.

Samuel gobbled down his piece and waited impatiently for Will to finish. "Mother said we don't have to work today, in honor of your birthday."

Will glanced at Mrs. Simpson, who nodded. She was a pretty woman, though tired-looking. Her eyes often had a sad, faraway look. But just then she looked at the boy and smiled. "It's been a blessing to have you with us, Will. Happy birthday."

Samuel now stood behind Will, beating a rhythm on the back of his chair with his hand. When the boy had forked in the last bite of cake, he pushed back the chair.

"Thanks," he said.

"My pleasure. Now you boys stay out of trouble," she urged, waving them off.

They picked up their fishing poles and gear and headed outside, letting the door slam behind them. Will hoped they'd fish from the pier, but Samuel wanted to take out the small boat. He knew a good spot to fish about half an hour away. So they headed to the wharf where his boat was tied.

After stowing their gear, Will climbed into the front of the boat. Samuel pushed off and jumped in as the boat rocked back and forth. They used their oars until they were far enough out in the bay to put up a sail. Samuel handed his friend the oars as he raised the canvas.

The wind picked up, and the small craft skimmed along the water, responding quickly to Samuel's every movement. Will closed his eyes and relaxed, for Samuel was a good sailor.

"We could run away," Will mused. "Then we'd never have to work again."

"I think I like my mother's cooking too much. And you could do worse than Mr. Spelman."

"That's true," Will agreed. "But let's not think of him this day. Let's think of fish—are we almost there?"

Samuel pointed toward land. "See that point?" They both stared at a rocky point that jutted out into the water. "I came here with my father once. We caught a basket of cod." His face looked sad.

"You miss him?" Will asked, for Samuel rarely talked about his father.

"Every day."

"How'd he die?"

"A storm came up," he began. "My pa couldn't make it home."

"But he'd been a fisherman a long time."

"Even a good sailor can't always predict storms," he answered with a shrug. "When the fog rolled in, we knew there was trouble. Ma and me waited all night—but it took a week for them to find his boat. They never did find his body."

The boys were silent for a minute. Will shivered as he stared into the inky water. He too remembered death at sea. Just then Samuel poked him with his oar. "Enough gloom. We're almost there."

They fished all afternoon, but Will's heart wasn't in it. Dark, sad memories had overcome him. Samuel didn't seem to notice. He completely filled his basket with cod, and only then did he notice his friend's silence.

"You didn't catch much."

"Guess I'm not much good at it," Will admitted. "But you caught enough for both of us."

"My mother will be pleased. She'll smoke them or salt them, and we'll be eating fish for a while."

As Samuel talked, he cleaned the fish, throwing the guts into the water. Gulls swarmed overhead, swooping down and carrying off the remains as the boys sailed off.

After supper Samuel begged his mother to let them go out. She protested weakly, but Samuel knew how to get what he wanted. He kept begging, and before long she had agreed that the two boys could go as long as they kept out of trouble.

As Will and Samuel stood on the front porch of the house, they heard noise coming from town. Samuel headed toward it, guided by the glow of an enormous bonfire. An edgy mob had gathered on King Street, fueled by strong drink freely handed out by Ebenezer Mackintosh and others. As usual, he had taken over as leader and stood before the people, egging them on.

Will felt a shiver of fear. It was an ugly mob, eager for trouble and needing little prompting from Mackintosh. Yet he seemed bound to stir it up even more. Will tugged at Samuel's sleeve. "We shouldn't stay. Look at them. They're out for blood, and something bad is going to happen."

"You're acting like a mother," Samuel hissed. "I'm not afraid. Look around you. All the men of Boston are here. Will you be a man? Or will you run back home like a girl?"

Will's ears burned. "You promised that you'd stay away from trouble," he reminded his friend.

Samuel scowled. "I'm not going to start trouble."

But he wouldn't avoid it either, Will knew. The two boys glared at each other, both itching for a fight.

"Where's Sam Adams? Where's Paul Revere?" Will asked.

"I don't care," Samuel muttered. "We're here, and I'm not slinking off."

"Look around you, fool. These men don't have anything

to lose if they get in trouble. They don't own land. They don't own businesses. Some don't even have jobs."

"So what? There's nothing wrong with being a sailor or a rope maker."

"Of course there isn't. But you don't follow 'em into battle, especially when you know how much it'll hurt your ma."

Loud voices drowned out the boys' words. Mackintosh had begun speaking. As he cursed the king and Thomas Hutchinson, the crowd whooped and hollered and pushed forward.

Will tugged at Samuel's sleeve. "Let's go."

"I won't!"

The crowd had worked itself into a frenzy. Drinks flowed freely, making even the timid bold and foolhardy. Samuel grabbed a tankard and gulped its contents down. It was almost impossible to hear the speakers, but that didn't much matter to the men who were already eager for action. As the mob surged forward, Will held Samuel back, trying to keep him from the center of things. The older boy shook the younger one off.

"Leave me be. I don't need a minder." Samuel's words slurred, and Will realized that his friend had had too much to drink, like most of those around them.

The crowd slowed. Suddenly Will saw weapons appearing. Clubs and sticks that had been hidden under shirts came out into the open. Rocks and bricks came out of pockets. Will nervously eyed the angry faces around him. When he turned back to Samuel, he found that his friend had slipped away, disappearing into the mob.

Suddenly everyone came to a complete stop. Will looked up. They were in front of the lieutenant governor's two-story brick house. "Hutchinson . . . Hutchinson . . ." The boy heard the lieutenant governor's name whispered about. As people realized where they were, their angry voices filled the air with curses and taunts. The mob was like a dry field, needing only a spark to catch fire. Ebenezer Mackintosh provided the spark.

"Men of Boston," he screamed, "how long will you let this schemer use his power and influence against you? His plotting puts money in his pocket and holes in yours. Look at this fine home. How many of you have glass in your windows and rich carpets on your floors?"

Angry murmurs rose and filled the air.

"It's not enough to talk and give speeches," Mackintosh continued. "Boston has too many speechmakers. Let them sit in their taverns and talk. We are men of action, men of courage. We will no longer take whatever scraps the king bestows." The lights within the house flickered off. Will realized that someone was inside, and he wondered who lived there with Mr. Hutchinson and if they were afraid.

Once the crowd grabbed hold of the word *traitor*, men tossed it back and forth until it became a roar. The next part happened so quickly that Will didn't see half of it. Men with broadaxes attacked the heavy oak front door, hacking their way through it. A rush of men pushed in from behind, flinging open shutters and smashing windows until the ground glittered with broken glass. Voices rose and fell in the still night air. Scraps of paper floated down from the broken windows.

Will froze, unable to move as the crowd in its fury turned the house into rubble. How could this happen to the king's man? Was the king so weak that he couldn't protect Thomas Hutchinson? If he was powerless against a mob in Boston, how could he be strong enough to protect the colonies from her enemies? In the midst of those thoughts he remembered his purpose: Find Samuel.

His friend wasn't among the men outside, who were battering the brickwork with stones and boards. Will didn't want to go inside because he was fearful of getting caught if the constable appeared. Yet he knew that's where Samuel was likely to be; so he forced himself to enter. Utter destruction met him. Not a piece of furniture remained whole. Once beautiful chairs had been destroyed, their legs and arms ripped from the seats, which lay on the floor like the dead on a battlefield. Broken china littered the rich carpet. Hutchinson's books and papers had borne the brunt of the mob's fury. Their torn pages covered every surface. Even the panels had been ripped from the walls.

And still the mob destroyed. In a daze Will wandered from room to room, and each time the scene was the same— men smashing, crushing, tearing, throwing anything they could get their hands on. Some men had fallen down drunk, but as soon as they fell, others filled their places. Will stumbled up the stairs, where he found Samuel in a bedroom about ready to smash a china lamp on a bedpost.

"Samuel!" he yelled.

His friend caught himself mid-swing. He looked at the lamp and then back at Will as though confused.

"What are you doing?" Will screamed again.

Slowly Samuel set the lamp down. After taking one last look around the room, he let Will drag him away. Though it took the boys twenty minutes to walk home, neither one said a word.

FIVE

During the night William Spelman returned home. He woke his apprentice early, rousing the boy from a troubled sleep and telling him to hurry to the shop.

Will tumbled from his bed, waking Samuel as he fell. The older boy moaned as he pulled a pillow over his head. Will dragged on his clothes and dashed down the stairs, stopping only long enough to grab a heel of bread left over from last night's supper.

His master was already at the shop when he arrived. Will couldn't remember that ever happening before, and he feared that it meant trouble. Mr. Spelman was pulling cases of type from shelves and shoving them into wooden crates. He'd even started taking apart the press.

"Master Spelman?"

"Yes, lad?"

"What are you doing?" Will feared his master had lost his mind.

"We're leaving this place," he explained, not bothering to look up from his task. "As soon as we're packed, we put Boston behind us."

"But why?"

The printer slammed a fist on the table. "Mobs are running the streets, and a person is no longer safe. What they did to Thomas Hutchinson's house was an outrage. They're lucky they didn't kill someone. This city will not live down its reputation as a scoundrel's refuge anytime soon."

"But how can you just leave?" Will demanded.

Spelman slumped onto a stool and shook his head. "I've lived in Boston all my adult life. It grieves me to see a city so changed and overcome by mobs. Though I never foresaw last night's action, I feared what might come. When I left town, it was to seek new opportunities—and I've found one. We will move the press to Worcester, away from this unrest, to a place where people have not yet lost their senses."

That was a long speech for Mr. Spelman, who was more given to grunts and nods.

"But what happens to me?" the boy asked.

"What do you mean?" he roared, hopping back to his feet. "You get to work. We have much to do here—and you will have much to do in Worcester."

"So I'm going with you?"

"Going with me?" he repeated as if Will had spoken in a foreign tongue. "Of course you're going with me. You belong to me—for six more years. And I aim to collect the work that's due me."

Will grinned, glad that he wouldn't once more be turned out on the street. Although he liked Boston, he didn't much care where he was going as long as he had a home. He'd known life as a beggar and as a printer's devil, and he much preferred the second.

Word spread quickly, and the shop was filled with folks eager to talk about the night's riots. Will listened intently, fearing that he might have been spotted.

"Poor Hutchinson. He was actually at home with his family just minutes before the mob arrived. He was convinced that the king's name could protect him," Doc Warren said, as he and Spelman smoked their pipes.

"Stubborn fellow," Sam Adams added. "If his daughter hadn't come back for him, who knows what might have happened? She slipped in from the back and persuaded him to flee just minutes before the mob broke through."

"His papers—his history of America—were destroyed. That's a true loss to all scholars," Adams said.

Though the visitors nodded to Will, none showed any signs of having seen him there. Gradually the boy relaxed, confident that his secret was safe from his master. Some of the men tried to convince Spelman to stay in Boston, but he merely shrugged and kept packing.

When the visitors left, his master locked the door behind them. "It's their fault," he said. "They may condemn the violence, but with their rash talk of independence, they encourage it."

The day rushed by as a blur. By evening the shop was empty. With the help of several strong men, the printer had carefully packed and loaded his heavy press onto a wagon. Canvas tarps covered it, and the load was tied on with strong rope. Only when Mr. Spelman knew the load was secure did he send Will home, and by then it was dark.

Samuel sulked at the table. Later when the boys went up to bed, Will tried to make him talk. "What's wrong with you?" he asked. "Was I the one who made you go to Hutchinson's house?"

Samuel glared at his friend and said nothing. His silence angered Will, who had an overwhelming urge to punch the other boy. Knowing it was the last time he would see Samuel for a long time, Will shook off the urge. He crawled into his bed and pulled the covers up. He was just drifting off to sleep when he heard a thump and felt Samuel nudge him.

"I'll miss you, Will Northaway."

"I'll miss you, too." Will felt a lump form in his throat. It was different leaving this time, for he had a friend and a family of sorts, but he knew he had no choice.

"Be careful," Will warned. "Mackintosh is a scoundrel."

"But at least he's brave. He's willing to fight the tyrant."

"What tyrant?" Will's anger flared again.

"The king, you fool."

"What did the king ever do to you?" Will couldn't keep the scorn from his voice. "You don't know anything but what a lot of angry people have told you. You're the reason we're leaving Boston, you and people like you. You say you hate the king, but all you're doing is hurting your neighbors."

Samuel didn't answer.

Will softened his tone. "If you really think the king is a tyrant," he said, "it would be better to make friends with Sam Adams and Paul Revere than to be hung with Mackintosh's mob."

Samuel laughed. "You may be right," he said. "I don't want to lose my head. I feel quite attached to it."

SIX

By the time the oxen were hitched to the heavily laden wagon, it was past nine. The sun was hot, and William Spelman's sweat-soaked shirt clung to his back. He was impatient to be off. Just as they were set to go, Will remembered that he'd left something at the rooming house.

"Will you wait?" he begged.

"What is it now?" Mr. Spelman asked.

"It won't take but a minute. I'll meet you at the Neck."

"See that you hurry," his master snapped. "We're already getting a late start, and if you're not there, I won't wait for you."

Will left him muttering under his breath. He found Mrs. Simpson washing clothes in the backyard. Since Will had already said good-bye to her and didn't want to go through that again, he dashed up the stairs, taking the steps two at a time. His bed had been stripped of its linens. The boy reached in his pocket and drew out a knife. Bending over, he etched his name into the wooden window sill and added the date, 1765. Then with one last look around the room that had been his refuge for the past year, he hightailed it to the Boston Neck.

The narrow sliver of land surrounded by water was the only way into and out of the city, except by boat. Sometimes after a storm the Neck was underwater. But the road today was so dry that a cloud of dust followed the wagon.

Will waited for his master to stop, but he merely tipped his hat and said, "You'd better get used to walking alongside. We want to spare the oxen." He clucked at the beasts, and the wagon lumbered past.

Will didn't have to hurry to keep up. The four oxen plodded so slowly that the boy could have run rings around the wagon and still kept pace. Instead, he plodded alongside the beasts.

Time dragged. Mr. Spelman rarely spoke. With the sun beating down on their heads, Will longed for a cool ocean breeze, but they were headed inland, away from the sea. The ground was hard beneath his feet. When they finally stopped to rest the oxen, Will threw himself under the shade of a tree.

"How much farther?" he asked.

Mr. Spelman grinned, his first smile all morning. "We've got days ahead of us," he replied.

The boy groaned. "Won't you miss the ocean?"

"P'raps," the printer grunted.

"But why Worcester?" Will persisted.

"They need a press. I need quiet."

They rested for a bit longer until the sun was not so high in the sky. Will thought it would be cooler, but when he realized they were now walking with the west-setting sun shining in their faces, he groaned again. Even the green pastures that lined the road on both sides did not give him pleasure. Occasionally a rider would pass them, but for the most part they had the road to themselves as they passed scattered farmhouses set amidst the fields.

By the end of the first day, they had gone six miles, stopping in a village with a church, a tavern, several shops, and a livery. They fed and stabled the oxen. Mr. Spelman took a room in the tavern, leaving Will to find a place in the hay. The boy ate the food his master had left him, took off his stiff boots, rubbed his aching feet, and fell asleep to the sounds of cattle lowing.

He slept soundly until awakened by his master's cheerful bray. "Wake up, lazybones."

Will rose up, stretching and brushing hay from his shirt and breeches. He stumbled out into the yard and washed his face in the water trough.

"Let's go," his master urged.

Will hobbled back into the barn and fetched his boots. His blistered feet protested as he shoved them in. By now his master had already hitched one pair of oxen to the wagon. Will yoked the other pair and led them out.

The beasts had eaten plenty of fresh hay and now chewed their cuds contentedly. Will felt his stomach rumble. He was hungry, but so far his master hadn't mentioned breakfast. He started to climb up on the wagon seat, but his master waved him off. "We must spare the beasts. Besides, the walking is good for you."

"At least the beasts have been fed," Will complained.

"I've got some cheese and bread for you," his master answered, pulling the food out of a leather satchel. "You might want to save some for later."

The day was hot and muggy. The sun beat down relentlessly. The air seemed thick enough to cut. The farther they went from Boston, the less traffic they saw on the road, and the worse the road was. The wagon bumped and rattled over the deep ruts, creaking at every pothole. From time to time Master Spelman looked back at the press to make sure it was secure.

By midday dark clouds began to form overhead. The wind picked up, blowing through the maples, tugging at their leaves and flipping them so that their underbellies flashed silver. The printer frowned.

"Check the ropes, lad. It's going to blow hard, and I want nothing to happen to my press."

Will barely had time to make sure the ropes were tight when the rain began to fall in huge drops. The sprinkle turned into a torrent, driving so hard that it became impossible for them to see the side of the road. They drew to a stop under an elm and waited out the storm. There was no protection for the animals, who bowed their heads as the rain beat down for hours.

Gradually the sky lightened, and the rain let up. Mr. Spelman jumped down from the wagon and inspected his load. He hiked ahead several yards, and when he came back, he looked worried.

"The road is muddy, and we'll be lucky not to lose a wheel. But we can't stay here. So let's hope for the best."

Once again Will checked the ropes. Now when he walked next to the wagon, thick clods of mud stuck to his boots. He walked carefully because it was hard to tell where the road was rutted. He didn't want to twist an ankle. His boots were soaked, as were his socks.

Keeping his eyes peeled for the next town, Will hoped they would soon be able to stop for the night. Though they passed farmhouses, it was nearly nightfall before he saw a steeple piercing the sky.

"Look!" he shouted. "A town."

Mr. Spelman looked up. "It's at least a mile off," he said with a frown. "Could be on the other side of the river."

He clucked at the soggy animals, urging them forward on the muddy road. The oxen slogged along, their heavy hooves sucking at the mud until they climbed a rise that offered a view of what lay ahead. "There it is," Master Spelman said grimly. "The river."

Will looked in the direction he was pointing and saw a glistening ribbon stretched across the horizon.

"It looks narrow enough," he said. "These strong beasts

should easily pull us through. And the town is not much farther on."

But as they plodded onward, the ribbon became a belt and then a sash.

"It looks as though the crossing may not be so easy." The printer wore a worried frown.

The road curved and dipped, and the river appeared and disappeared from their sight. Finally they were close enough to hear the roar of rushing water. Then it appeared, a slash of water frothing and churning and spilling over its banks. Master Spelman drew the oxen to a halt and set the brake. He looked upstream and down, chewing his lip as he considered what to do.

"Will we cross tonight?" Will asked. "It's getting dark." Though they had not run into many travelers, especially after the rain, Will knew there were dangers on the highway. Robbers could prey on travelers unfortunate enough to be caught off guard. He knew his master would feel better if they had reached the next town.

"I know it's dark," Mr. Spelman snapped, hopping down from the wagon and striding to the river. It was only twenty feet across, but it flowed so swiftly that it might as well have been a mile. "We won't ever make it across," he finally said. "My press will end up at the bottom if we try." Will kept silent as his master continued, "If it rains again, it will only get worse. If we go . . . well, we both know the risk."

As Mr. Spelman paced and worried, darkness crept across the sky. He looked up with a startled expression. "It seems God has made our decision for us," he muttered, signaling Will to begin unyoking the oxen.

After watering them, Will tied them loosely in a patch of thick grass well away from the rushing water. Supper was a cold one—dried meat and stale biscuits—but neither complained. When it was time for bed, Will curled up on a tarp under the wagon. His master found a dry corner inside it.

Will woke during the night to the soft sound of rain peppering the grass, but when he awoke in the morning, it had passed. A blue sky promised a good day if they could safely cross the river. He rolled out from under the wagon and staggered to the water's edge. The river still ran swiftly, but the bottom was now visible in places. He walked up and down the bank, trying to determine the best place to cross.

"How does it look?" Mr. Spelman's voice took Will by surprise.

Will whirled around, stick in hand, and shrugged. "Seems most shallow over there where it's widest."

Spelman scowled. "If I had a horse, I'd ride out and test the depth. As it is, how can we know? It may be shallow near the banks, but the storm could have dug a channel in the middle."

They both stood and watched the swiftly flowing river. "We'll go here," the printer finally said, pointing to a spot that was neither wide nor narrow.

Will shrugged but didn't argue as the oxen chewed their cuds. "Dumb beasts," the boy muttered. "You'll go to whatever fool place my master leads you."

When the animals were yoked, Master Spelman checked the ropes securing the press. He tested the wheels, and when he was satisfied, they set off. The wagon bumped down the slope to the stream's edge, gathering a bit of speed. The animals hesitated, but when Master Spelman pulled out his whip and snapped it over their backs, the first two oxen lunged into the water, which reached midway up their legs. They paused to get their footing before pushing forward. The second pair, trained to follow, plunged in behind them. Will followed the animals into the stream, gasping as the cold water soaked through his clothes. He held onto the wagon, ready to act if the load began to tip.

The beasts lurched forward, dragging the bulky wagon into the stream. It tipped, rocking a bit from side to side, before settling into the water. Will gripped its side to steady himself. The strong current threatened to tear the boy from the wagon and send him rushing downstream like a broken branch. He hadn't taken more than five steps when the water reached his waist. It was neck deep on the oxen, who strained to keep their heads above water.

The heavy press weighed the wagon down. Its wheels bumped and scraped along the bottom before coming to a halt. As the oxen kept pulling, the wagon groaned and shuddered.

"It's stuck!" Will shouted.

"Whoa, whoa," Master Spelman yelled at the beasts, who were desperately pulling as the water lapped around their necks.

Crack! The wagon jerked forward and then leaned to the right. Will hung on to the side with both hands, hoping he wouldn't be swept downstream before his master ever noticed.

The load shifted. Water rushed over the top of the wagon, threatening to sweep the chests and barrels away. Will clung to the wagon as his legs crashed into submerged rocks. The first team of oxen slipped, and one of the beasts went under. Suddenly the two teams were no longer pulling together. Instead, each beast was scrambling for his own foothold. They hit another rock, and several barrels tumbled into the stream. Will watched them float away.

The water carried the wagon downstream a bit, and then suddenly the oxen found their footing and began to pull as they'd been trained. When they reached the far bank, the beasts climbed out.

Will threw himself exhaustedly on the bank. His leg throbbed, but he didn't even have the strength to look at it. Mr. Spelman hopped down from the wagon and surveyed the damage. One wheel was completely destroyed. Another had several broken spokes. Meanwhile they'd lost at least two barrels and a crate.

The printer sat down on the bank and pressed his head between his hands. Will looked over at him and thought the man was crying. Embarrassed, he turned away and examined his leg. An ugly gash ran across his calf. Blood flowed freely from the wound. He tore a bit of cloth from the bottom of his shirt and wrapped it tightly around his leg to stop the bleeding.

By this time his master was on his feet. "We'll have to repair the wagon. I've got one spare wheel. If we're careful, we can make it to town and then repair the other one."

Will pointed downstream where the barrels had disappeared. "Should I see if they've swept ashore?"

His master nodded wearily. "Couldn't hurt. But if you don't see them by the bend in the river, come back."

Will limped along the river, scanning the banks for the cargo. He saw logs, twigs, and long grasses caught along the banks, but no crates or barrels. He'd almost reached the bend when he saw something glittering. He scrambled down, climbing over tree roots, and reached into the water. Some underwater roots had snagged a case of type. Though the boy searched further, that was all he found.

He carried back his trophy, wincing every time he put weight on his leg. Master Spelman looked up at the sound of the boy's approach. "Is that all?" he asked.

"It was caught in some roots," the boy answered. "But I couldn't find the rest."

His master sighed. Type was expensive. It would take a

long time to replace the day's losses. He closed his eyes again, and Will set the waterlogged case in the wagon. He was tired and wanted nothing more than to reach town and go to bed. But first they had to fix the wheel. Together, the boy and his master removed what was left of the old wheel and put on the new.

"I should not have been so rash," the printer said, rubbing a hand across his unshaven jaw.

"What happened to your hand?" Will asked.

The man looked down at the angry red burns on his palms as though noticing them for the first time. "Must have been the reins," he mused. "The oxen about pulled my arms out of the sockets."

"I thought we were lost." Will looked back at the swiftly running stream and felt pride stir within. "But we didn't do too badly."

"Don't spend too much time congratulating yourself, lad. We could have lost everything. Even our lives."

"But we didn't!"

"You're right. We didn't, and maybe we should thank God for that."

Will shrugged. It didn't much matter to him whom they thanked. He was grateful to be on land, and even the burning cut on his leg couldn't dampen his pleasure.

When they'd finished the repairs, Mr. Spelman pulled out the last of their food and gave some to his apprentice. Then they filled their bottles with water and set off, grateful to have the river behind them and a good road ahead.

SEVEN

Will's throbbing leg kept him from falling asleep. Though he was tired from the day's journey, he tossed and turned all night. In the morning a wet tongue awoke him. Through half-opened eyes he glimpsed a shaggy black and white dog standing over him, his scrawny tail wagging.

Will groaned, pushed the dog away, and pulled the blanket over his head. But the dog tugged at the blanket as though he were playing tug of war.

"Who are you?" Will groaned.

The dog, tongue hanging and tail thumping, sat down and cocked his head.

"Not going to answer? That's okay. I can guess that you're hungry. Me too. But you've come to the wrong place. I have no food, and my master won't want to share with you." As the boy talked, the dog's tail thumped more enthusiastically.

Will looked up the street, hoping to catch sight of his master, who had again spent the night in a tavern. He spotted him about halfway down the street. "There's our master," he said to the dog. "He's got breakfast. If you don't make a pest of yourself, I'll share a bit of mine with you."

The dog danced around the boy's feet as though he understood everything he'd said. Before Mr. Spelman reached the livery stable, the dog had dashed out of the barn, barking and grinning at the printer.

"Whose dog?"

"He woke me up this morning. He's beautiful, isn't he?"

"He is a good-looking dog," the printer agreed. "But I don't have time for such nonsense. Let's get these beasts yoked."

As the boy led the oxen over, he pestered his master. "Can I keep him?"

"He must belong to someone."

"But if he doesn't?"

A look of irritation passed over the printer's face. Before he could speak, the boy interrupted. "We could use a watchdog. He could warn us of bandits or redcoats."

"Or patriots like Mackintosh," Mr. Spelman added as he scratched the back of his head. "No harm in asking around. If he doesn't belong to anyone, you can keep him— as long as he's no trouble. Do you understand?"

Will nodded, too happy to speak. When the printer handed him his cold meat pie, the boy immediately broke off a piece and fed it to the dog. The animal wolfed it down in a single gulp before looking up and begging for more.

"What will you call him?"

"Can't decide now. I have to wait and see if he's mine," the boy answered.

When the oxen were yoked, they headed through town with the dog prancing alongside the wagon. At the tavern they stopped and asked about him.

"I've never seen him before," the tavern keeper told a grinning Will.

"Then come on, boy," Mr. Spelman urged. "We've got miles to go before we rest."

The dog made the time go faster. He darted after rabbits and barked at birds, whose shadows flittered over the grass. Sometimes the dog ran so far afield that Will feared he wouldn't come back. Then he'd hear joyful barking, and the dog would reappear, wagging tail and all.

Even the dog, though, couldn't keep the trip from being tiresome. By the fourth day, the boy had wearied of traveling, and his leg continued to hurt. Every day was the same as the wagon wound through rolling hills and around farms and orchards. Some days were a little longer, some shorter, depending on how far it was from town to town. Each day Will and his master scanned the horizon for the steeples that marked the next one.

"I never thought I'd be so eager to see a church," Will said when he spied a steeple midway through one afternoon.

"We haven't had much use for churches, have we, Will?"

"That's been fine with me."

"But it shouldn't be. I promised Mr. Mattison that I'd see to your religious education. It's even in the contract I signed."

"You've taken me to church."

"I have to. It's the law." The printer scratched his jaw.

"It's enough. We're doing fine."

Mr. Spelman was quiet as the wagon rumbled on. Just then the dog darted into a field dotted with sheep. He began barking and nipping at the legs of the woolly creatures until they began to run, baaing loudly. Within minutes the sheep were huddled in the center of the field, and the dog was wagging his tail at the wagon.

"Did you see that?" the boy began.

"He's quite a sheepdog," Mr. Spelman said. "Perhaps you should name him David."

"Why is that?"

"Most famous shepherd in the Bible," his master answered. "Don't tell me you don't know that."

Will looked shamefaced as he shook his head. He'd just given his master a further excuse to talk about church, and the boy had no interest. He kept silent, figuring the best he could do was to hope his master would forget.

He knew it wasn't likely, for a change had come over Spelman, one Will had first noticed after the river crossing. He'd caught the printer praying silently as the wagon rolled along the rutted track. At first when he'd seen his master's gently swaying body, he'd thought he was sleeping and wondered if he would topple to the ground. But when that didn't happen, he realized his master wasn't asleep, but was instead praying. Now this talk about church added to his fears. Something was going on, and the boy wasn't sure that he liked it.

EIGHT

They rolled into Worcester on a clear, moonlit night. The town was dark except for light flickering in the windows of the few houses that surrounded the square. Freshly mown hay perfumed the air.

Worcester was a small farming town. Two streets bordered the Green. The church sat on one end of town, the town hall on the other. In between were a few shops and taverns. The boy and his master unhitched the oxen in front of an empty shop the printer had rented. Then Will led them to the livery where he unyoked them and settled them for the night.

A storm came through during the night, bringing with it cold, damp air that seeped through the doors and windows of the unheated house. When Will woke, his bones ached. He heard voices outside and stumbled to the window. A small crowd had gathered around the wagon.

Mr. Spelman was already outside speaking to the neighbors. As Will pulled on his breeches, the printer pushed open the door. "Hurry up, lad. We've much work to do. It all must be unloaded before the Lord's Day."

After pulling on his coat, Will hurried outside. It was market day. The streets were full of wagons, and farmers, curious about the newcomers, wandered over to look at the press. As he helped unload the wagon, Will examined them. They were plain folk, dressed in rough cloth meant for outdoor work rather than for style.

When it was time to move the press, they readily joined

in, lifting the heavy machine and carrying it into the shop. As they worked, they peppered the printer with questions about Boston, the roads, and politics.

"We've never had a press in Worcester," said an old man standing to the side.

"You've got one now," Mr. Spelman answered cheerfully. "I print books, handbills, whatever needs doing. I won't turn away an honest dollar."

"That might be hard to come by," another man remarked. "We've had better years. There's not much money floating around."

"Nor in Boston," Mr. Spelman said. "It's never good for business when there's unrest, but I'm a patient man. I trust we can prosper here."

"Our problem is not unrest," the farmer said, shaking his head. "It's debt. We borrowed money for nails and seed in the spring, but dry weather and pests have hurt the crops, and most of us won't harvest enough to pay the money back."

"That's right," another farmer agreed, pushing forward. "And if we don't bring in a good harvest, these merchants won't be selling us goods, and they'll be owing money in Boston."

For several minutes the farmers argued among themselves about the cause of the problem. Finally, since the wagon was empty, Mr. Spelman interrupted their talk. "Thank you for your kind help. I'm sure I'll see you again."

"Aye. You're welcome." The farmers began to drift away in small groups, still grumbling about their crops and predicting worse things to come. Will followed his master inside and began to help him put the heavy press back together. Before long his master looked out at the darkening sky. "We'll need to buy some things," he said. Pulling out a few coins from his pocket, he handed them to the boy. "Eggs, cornmeal, salt, bacon, and milk. That should tide us over for a few days."

Will set off with a milk jug and basket, eager to see a bit of the town. "I'll not call you David," he said to the dog skipping alongside him.

He studied the dog's black and white face, perky ears, and pointed snout. "Black and white—you look a bit like my printing. I guess I'll call you Ink and be done with it. Now you'd better behave. No chasing anyone's chickens."

The town was so small that it took Will less than half an hour to walk around it. Maple trees displaying yellow, orange, and red leaves surrounded the freshly whitewashed church, the largest building in the square. In the shadow of its bell tower stood small shops. Farm wagons full of pumpkins, apples, pears, squash, and corn clustered on the Green. Will walked from wagon to wagon until he had filled his jug with milk and his basket with eggs and bacon. Ink, smelling the bacon through its paper wrapping, stuck close to the boy, hoping for a bite.

Will could imagine his master busily putting together the press and finding places for the type, paper, and inks. And though he knew he should return, he didn't feel like working inside. He glanced at the jug of milk and heavily laden basket.

A young woman watched him from her wagon. "I've not seen you before."

"We just arrived. I'm the printer's lad."

"Ah, yes. We'd heard a printer was coming. From Boston, isn't he?"

"Yes, ma'am."

"That's a long way to come. What do you think of your new home?"

Will shrugged. "I haven't seen much of it."

"It's a beautiful day. You should explore a bit."

Will looked regretfully down at his bundles.

"I'll watch them for you. We'll be here until four." Will hesitated for an instant, but the woman urged him on. "Go on . . ."

"My name's Will," he said.

"Well then, you go on, Will. Your groceries will be here when you come back."

Will didn't wait for her to repeat the invitation. He whistled at Ink, and together they loped away from the village toward golden fields of corn and a far-off stand of trees. Mowers were cutting the last of the hay. Dry leaves crackled under his feet; smoke rose from piles of burning leaves. When he plucked an apple from a low-hanging branch and took a bite, sweet juice dripped down his chin.

Will thought of Samuel. It would be nice to have him around, but at least he had Ink. He filled his pockets with walnuts that lay thick underfoot and pitched acorns at Ink, who chased and bit them before spitting out the bitter pieces. Although the boy soon grew weary of the game, the dog kept bringing sticks to him.

"Go on. Go chase a squirrel. I'm tired of throwing things for you."

Ink sat down and grinned while Will stalked off in the opposite direction. The boy knew he ought to head back; so he whistled and began walking, heading back toward town where the tip of the church steeple was barely visible above the trees.

Will had reached the edge of town when someone said, "You're the printer's devil, aren't you?"

He looked up to see a thick lad standing in the middle of the road, an axe slung over his shoulder.

"News travels quickly here. We just arrived."

The boy didn't return Will's smile. "How's your master expect to work? When November comes, there won't be any business for a printer—unless he uses stamped paper. And if he does, we'll run him out of town."

"And if he doesn't use stamped paper?"

"He'd be breaking the law. The king's men won't let him get away with that."

"How do you know this?"

"My master explained it to me. Why don't you go and ask your master if it's true."

Will chewed on his lip. Why hadn't his master explained things to him? What were they going to do? He kicked at the ground and then remembered the other apprentice, who was still staring at him.

"I've got to go," Will mumbled. "I'm already late."

"Ask your master," the other boy laughed. "Then you might as well take yourselves back to Boston."

Without a backward glance, Will trotted over to the Green, wondering where Ink had gone. He gathered his parcels from the farmer's daughter and ran to the printer's shop.

"You're late." Master Spelman looked up from his work as the boy dashed into the shop.

"Sorry."

"Don't bother to take off your coat. We still need wood. You better split some and bring it inside. Looks like rain."

Will sighed, picked up the axe, and headed out the door.

NINE

In many ways Will's life in Worcester was like his life in Boston. He still rose early to start the fire and draw the water. During the day he mixed ink, sorted type, hung pages to dry, cleaned the press, delivered orders, scrubbed the floor, cut wood, went to the market, and did whatever else his master told him to do.

Will missed Mrs. Simpson's cooking. Now it was his job in the morning to make breakfast, and after a long day of work, it was his job to cook supper. Though he wasn't much of a cook, they did not starve.

Mr. Spelman often went out to the taverns at night so that he could meet the men of Worcester. "More business gets done over a tankard of ale or cider than anywhere else," he explained to the boy. "They must come to trust me, or I'll get no business from them."

"But how will you do business after November 1?" Will asked. "The Stamp Tax will keep you from printing. You'll have to decide whose side you're on."

"Aye, I'll have to decide," the printer agreed. "But so will every other printer in the colonies. There's still time."

Will noticed that his master often paused from his work to search the Bible, which he now kept on his desk. Then one night after they had eaten dinner, his master called the boy to him. "Sit with me, lad."

"But aren't you going out?" Will protested.

"Not tonight. I've got to keep a long-delayed promise."

Will eyed his master warily as he pulled another chair close to the fire.

"Let us fix some tea and get comfortable," Mr. Spelman said, pouring the hot water into the pot. When the tea had steeped, he poured it with a little milk into two cups. Then he sat back with his big Bible on his knee and said, "Let's read."

Will tried not to doze off as his master read, but the warmth of the fire and the lateness of the hour combined to put the tired boy to sleep. So the next day his master stopped work an hour earlier.

"But it's only five o'clock," Will said.

"If we're going to squeeze our Bible reading in before you fall asleep, we'd better begin earlier."

As Will bustled about the fire preparing cornbread and ham for supper, his master read. At first he was angry and didn't want to listen. Over time, however, the stories began to interest him. How did Adam feel when his son Cain killed his other son Abel? How did Ishmael feel when his father sent him away? Or Isaac, when his father held a knife to his throat?

Will began to look forward to the daily reading. Even when his master went out, which he still did from time to time, he managed to squeeze in a chapter before he went. Though Will had expected to hear dull stories about holy people floating on clouds in the sky, his master read him adventure stories full of characters like Isaac, who blessed the wrong son, and Jacob, who loved Joseph best, and Joseph's brothers, who became so jealous of their brother they tried to kill him.

As the days shortened and the temperatures fell, politics came to the front of everyone's thinking. One night after they'd read a chapter, Will looked at his master and asked, "What will you do?"

Mr. Spelman rubbed his temples. His forehead creased with worry. "I don't know. I can't afford to stop the press for a year. How will I pay my bills?"

"I guess you could borrow like the farmers do," Will replied. "They owe everyone in town."

"But I'm a stranger here. No one knows me well. They don't know that I will pay them back."

"But you own the press. It's worth something."

"It's worth a great deal, son. I would not want to lose it."

As November 1 drew near, Mr. Spelman began going every night to the tavern, as eager as any farmer for news from Boston. He hoped the king had changed his mind about the tax. But if he didn't, the printer was determined to support the king. It was not a popular position. The small farmers hated taxes. They were barely making ends meet, and they could not afford to pay any more to the king across the sea.

Mr. Spelman kept his opinions quiet. Like most of the town, he watched and waited, hoping something would happen to prevent trouble. His silence made some neighbors suspicious. If he agreed with them, why didn't he say so?

One day Will came home and found a fine carriage tied in front of the shop. When he opened the door, he found his master huddled in the back with two well-dressed squires, whose expensive boots gleamed. They didn't stay long, and when they left, Will watched their shiny black carriage drive off. Neighbors stared as it drove down the middle of the narrow street. A few took off their hats, but most turned their backs on it.

"Who was that?"

"John Chandler and Timothy Paine," his master said.

"They must be important. I've never seen such a fine carriage except in London."

"Probably the two richest men in the county. Well-respected, decent men. You must always show respect to them."

Will shrugged. "Did they bring business?"

"Not today but perhaps in the future. We found we have many common interests."

Will's face was still red from the cold. He rubbed his hands together in front of the fire. "Everyone is talking about what happened at the Stamp Tax congress."

"What do you mean?" asked his master.

"General Ruggles refused to sign the statement declaring that the colonies are against the tax."

"I'm glad someone is willing to stand for reason. Why should Massachusetts set itself against the king?"

"But the town folk are furious. They say he betrayed the cause. The people of Massachusetts sent him to the congress; so he should have signed it. And since he was president of the congress, the meeting ended without a statement."

"We can be thankful he showed courage. Think of the pressure that was put on him," Mr. Spelman said.

Will felt anger bubbling up inside. "Why should one man have so much power? Everyone says he was wrong. He should have signed."

Mr. Spelman leaned back on his stool and stretched out the muscles of his back. "If he believed strongly that the statement was wrong, he had a duty to refuse to sign."

"Even if the people who sent him wanted him to?"

"Even then. He's wiser than they are and must make these decisions according to his wisdom."

"They say he was afraid to anger the governor, that's all. But he'll have to choose who to serve, the people or the king."

"Perhaps he'll choose to serve God," Mr. Spelman said, looking fondly at his apprentice. "You seem to be spending a lot of time listening to everybody. Perhaps you should spend a bit more time trying to determine your own proper course."

"I'm only an apprentice. What difference does it make? I have no power or vote."

"Which reminds me, there's a town meeting tonight. I plan to go; so you'll have to lock up."

"Will you speak?" Will looked anxiously at his master. It was one thing to talk about General Ruggles, but he feared his master would say something to anger his neighbors.

"I plan to listen, but I'll not let a mob keep me from speaking."

As Mr. Spelman went out, a cold drizzle fell, bringing down leaves with it. They formed a sodden mess underfoot. "Don't wait up for me," he said, pulling a scarf up around his chin.

Will anxiously watched his master walk down the street, grieving the loss of the short peace they had enjoyed. He knew his master would argue for the king's side, and he knew it would mean trouble. How the boy wished they could move far away from Worcester—far away from all talk of taxes.

Will went out early the next day, eager to hear about the night's meeting. In the general store and the apothecary men talked of little else. The town had voted that its representative to the legislature should not support the Stamp Tax. Mr. Paine and Mr. Chandler had urged the town to obey the law. So had Will's master. In a fiery speech he had attacked those who would not obey the king's authority. When the boy heard the report, he ran from the store, trying to avoid anyone who might recognize him.

TEN

Will's master didn't talk much about the town meeting. Several times the boy saw him in deep conversation with Mr. Chandler or Mr. Paine, but when Will asked what they were discussing, his master clammed up. "It's better if you don't know."

Will knew that meant trouble. He didn't know from which direction trouble would come. On November 1 when he arose and saw the gray skies, he felt as gloomy as the weather. His master was up early and already had the press working. It was a small order, by the looks of it. Half a dozen pages hung from the line to dry.

"Go ahead and wash the plates," his master ordered. "We may not need them for a while."

Will scrubbed the inky plates and rollers in the powerful lye solution. It burned his hands and left them sore and inky. Meanwhile his master put away his tools and took out the large Bible, which he began to read. Will knew something was going on. His master wore a determined look, and though the big book was open on his lap, he seemed to be thinking of something else.

When the printed pages had dried, Mr. Spelman wrapped them in plain brown paper and tied them with a piece of twine. "Take these to Mr. Chandler," he said. "Be quick about it, for he is waiting for them."

"I didn't know he had given you business," Will said, chewing the inside of his cheek.

"No questions. Just be about your business. Don't stop to chat."

Will frowned. "Isn't this November 1?" he asked.

"Yes . . ."

"I thought you couldn't print stuff without the king's stamp."

Mr. Spelman's face turned purple. "I told you what to do. I'll not have a mere lad question me."

Will hurried out the door, carrying the unwanted parcel under his arm. He wasn't sure what it held because he hadn't been able to read the printing. He took the back way around town and rested only when he reached the path heading out toward Chandler's farm. It was a mile walk, which was nothing to the boy. The dog pranced eagerly at his side.

"Go on, catch us a hare for supper," he said, rubbing the shepherd's ears. He watched the dog run off in pursuit of a critter the boy could not see. He was so busy watching the dog and listening to the birds that he didn't notice a boy blocking the path ahead.

"What do you have there?"

Startled, Will looked up. Standing in front of him was the same boy who had warned him before.

"Who are you?" Will asked. "You never told me."

When the boy didn't answer, Will pressed on. "Who's your master?"

"Mr. Veree, the hooper," the other lad answered grudgingly.

Will nodded and tried to walk past, but the boy blocked his way.

"Move!" Will cried angrily.

"You work for that Tory printer, don't you?"

Will shrugged and tried to push past.

"Everyone knows he took the side of Chandler and Paine. The River Kings, we call them. They think they own this town, but things are changing, and they won't control it much longer. Your master will regret his vote."

Will felt a nervous flutter in the pit of his stomach. He had expected trouble but not so soon. Again he tried to push past the boy, but the larger lad grabbed him by the coat collar and threw him down, sending his parcel flying onto the wet ground. The hooper's boy scrambled to pick it up.

"Leave that alone! It belongs to my master," Will screamed as the other boy tore the wrapping off the package. Pages of print floated to the ground. Will lunged for them, but the other boy was stronger and threw him aside. Then the hooper's boy bent over and picked up one of the handbills.

"Look at this," he sneered. "The king's stamp. I guess that answers the question about what side your master is on. He paid the tax on this paper. The proof is right there." He pointed at the corner where a stamp and seal showed payment of the tax.

Will struggled to stand up. "So he obeyed the law. Is that now a crime in Massachusetts?"

"But that's the whole question. Whose law will we obey? Your master has made his choice. Now it's time for you to make yours."

Will watched the boy take a step toward him. Before Will could scramble to his feet, the other boy was upon him. His greater size and weight allowed him to pin the printer's boy and land several punches to his face. Blood spurted from Will's nose and dripped onto the wet ground.

"The men of Worcester don't like Tories," the hooper's boy growled. "You go home and say that."

Will wiped his nose with the back of his hand. "You'd better watch yourself. My master has powerful friends."

"I wouldn't count on those friends," the boy sneered as he lumbered away. "Their time has come and gone."

Will bent down to pick up the few handbills that the other boy had left behind. They were muddy and good for nothing, but at least they wouldn't provide any more ammunition for his master's enemies.

Will wasn't sure which way to go. Ahead Mr. Chandler waited for the package. It would not be good to anger such a powerful man. Behind him waited his master, who would be furious when he heard what had happened to his package. As Will was thinking, Ink bounded out of the woods, his coat covered with burrs. From his jaws hung the limp body of a rabbit.

The dog pranced proudly at his master's feet. The boy rubbed his ears and gently pried the rabbit from his jaws. "Perhaps this will take away our master's anger," he said. "In any case, we must go home and face the music. But there'll be a price to pay."

They found Mr. Spelman reading his Bible and staring out the window. He looked up with relief when he heard the boy come in, but when he saw his bloodstained shirt and muddy clothes, his face clouded over.

"What happened?"

"It wasn't my fault," Will began. "The hooper's lad knocked me down and took the printing . . . all except for this." Will held out the few muddy sheets that he had rescued.

"He knocked you down?"

"Said the town doesn't like Tories. He'd heard about your speech at the town meeting."

"This must be stopped. I'll talk to his master and demand that he pay for the damage."

"Please don't," Will begged. "For all you know, he was doing what his master commanded."

"Has lawlessness stretched its arm all the way to Worcester?"

Will said nothing. He stared at the wooden plank floor and wished it would open and gobble him up.

Mr. Spelman paced the small room, stopping occasionally to slap the table as Will inched over to the fireplace where the heat slowly began to dry his clothes.

"Did he hurt you?" his master asked suddenly, as though Will's bloody nose had only then come to his attention.

"Not too much," the boy answered. "It could have been worse."

ELEVEN

It was a lonely winter. Heavy snow kept many farmers close to home, and Mr. Spelman rarely ventured out, except for church and an occasional stop at the tavern. He entertained rarely, and then just a few trusted friends.

Though most townsmen were not hostile, they were not friendly either. They spent their days dealing with their own problems and had little energy left over to worry about the king or his taxes. As the snow piled up in drifts outside their windows and doors, and as people put away their wagons and pulled out their sleighs, Will felt as though all of Worcester had gone into hibernation.

Money was scarce. Mr. Spelman had shut down his press, for his neighbors had made it clear that they would not pay for stamped paper, and the printer would not print without it. Since there was little money to buy food, it rested upon them to catch it. Will's master taught the boy how to shoot and clean the musket, and he was content to let the boy go hunting.

Will was more than happy with his new duties. Bundled in an old deerskin coat belonging to his master, he crisscrossed fields on his snowshoes in search of game. At his side, Ink would prance and play in the new-fallen snow.

"Find us a rabbit or some squirrels," Will commanded Ink.

As if he understood, the black and white dog, often chest high in snow, willingly bounded off in every direction, his eager barks directing the boy to a burrow or squirrel.

One morning the boy woke up and discovered that their cupboard was nearly empty. Except for a bit of sugar and cornmeal, a few vegetables, and a pound of bacon, nothing remained for them to eat.

"We must either go to market or bring in some game," Mr. Spelman said.

Will noted his master's worried frown and realized that it had become all too familiar.

"We'll go. Ink and I haven't been out for some time," Will offered.

"But look at the clouds. A storm is brewing."

"Don't worry. We won't go far."

Because he didn't really have another choice, Mr. Spelman bade the boy go and watched as he put on his coat and grabbed the musket and game bag. From the window he watched him strap on the snowshoes. Will turned and waved before plunging into the drifts.

Smoke drifted up from the chimneys, and the sweet smell of burning apple wood filled the air. The cold bit into the boy's cheeks. As the snow soaked his boots, his feet ached from the cold. "We must hurry, Ink. No time to play today. Storm's coming, and it's already cold."

For more than an hour they wandered in search of small game, following rabbit tracks across the snow without finding the animal. All the while the clouds thickened. Before long, snow began gently to fall.

By this time the boy was nearly frozen, but he was determined to bring home something to eat. He plunged into the woods where the snow, blocked by trees, was less deep, and he could move more quickly. He scanned the ground in vain and was about to admit defeat and head back to town when Ink began barking and darted away into a thick stand of trees.

Will plowed after him, hoping the dog would be able to catch whatever he was chasing. He followed the dog's path as it zigzagged through the trees. Ahead the sound of Ink's excited barking drew him on.

Will stopped to catch his breath. He checked the musket at his side and saw that it was ready to shoot. Pushing away thoughts about the snow or the cold, he plunged on. The dog's yelps had become faint, and Will rushed to catch up. A couple of steps farther, the barking stopped. Will stopped and listened, but the woods were deathly silent except for the rasping of his own breath in his ears.

"Ink! Ink!" His screams were met with silence. Fear struck, and the boy shouted again, but he heard no answer. Then came the sound of something crashing through the woods.

The boy ran toward the sound. "Ink," he screamed. The crashing grew faint as though someone was running away.

"Who is it?" the boy yelled.

No one answered. The boy raised his musket and plunged blindly ahead. "Stop, or I'll shoot," he yelled. Whatever or whoever had made the crashing sound had gone. Will could hear nothing except his own breathing.

He continued more slowly toward the place he thought he'd first heard the sound, calling out the dog's name.

Finally he heard a whimper. Tears sprang to his eyes. "Ink," he gasped, pushing through the trees. He stopped abruptly when he came upon blood-splattered ground. Human footprints trailed off one way, and a small bloody track led in another.

"Ink?"

Again the boy heard a whimper. He followed the bloody trail for ten paces and found the dog collapsed in a pile at the base of an ancient oak. Will kneeled beside his wounded pet.

"What happened, boy? Who did this to you?"

The dog tried to lift his head, but he was too injured. His tail thumped weakly on the snow. Will touched Ink gently, being careful as he probed. The dog licked his hand once, and then he went limp.

Will continued to probe with fingers, saying, "Shh . . . shh," to calm the anxious dog. The dog's head was matted, and when Will pulled his fingers away, they were sticky with blood. He began to shiver as he became aware of the cold seeping through his wet clothes. Cradling the dog in his arms, he lifted him and turned to go. "Don't die," he commanded the dog. "Don't die."

The boy stumbled under the weight of his pet. Then he realized that the animal was no longer whimpering. He lowered his head to listen for any sign of life, but Ink had stopped breathing. His body hung limply in Will's arms.

"Who did this?" Will muttered. As he questioned, anger rushed through him. He set the body down and headed back to the spot where he'd first seen blood. A human trail clearly led into the woods. He searched a bit more and found a bloody rock. Will picked it up and stuck it in his pocket.

He intended to follow the trail, but first he needed to bury the body. Since he couldn't dig into the frozen ground, he did his best to bury his pet under a mound of rocks, hoping they would be enough to protect Ink from wolves and other animals. When done, he wiped away the tears that continued to drip down his cheeks and snowshoed back to the place where the dog had been injured.

At this point the boy had no idea how far he had traveled or how long he'd been gone, and he didn't care. He was determined to follow the track and find the dog's killers.

The trail was easy to follow at first. Its makers had done nothing to hide their tracks. It led out of the woods and across a field. The snow began to fall at a pace that would soon cover the trail. Will hurried, but the tracks only led back to town where they had been erased by traffic and drifting snow.

"If only I had Ink to help." The thought brought tears to his eyes.

Just then three boys appeared. "Hey, it's the printer's boy," one of them said.

"You're right about that," said another.

Will didn't recognize two of the boys, but the third, the one who hadn't yet spoken, was the hooper's apprentice. All three of them glared at Will.

"Where's your dog?" one of the boys sneered.

"What do you know about my dog?" Will demanded. His hand clutched the wooden stock of his musket.

The hooper's boy shrugged, but one of the others couldn't hide a smirk. Clenching his fists, Will took a step toward him, and the boy inched back.

Just then the hooper strode down the road. "I've been looking all over for you, lad." He grabbed his apprentice by the collar with one hand and cuffed his ear with the other. "Where have you been?"

The two other boys melted away, leaving the hooper's boy on his own to deal with his angry master. "I was just out with my friends," he muttered.

"Speak up!" The hooper cuffed him again. "I sent you to the store, and you were gone for hours."

The apprentice looked sideways at Will, clearly wishing he would leave.

"And what's that all over you?" The hooper peered at his boy's coat. "Well? What is it? Speak up!" And he cuffed him again.

Will almost felt sorry for the boy until he heard him mutter in a near whisper, "It's blood."

"Blood! Blood! From where? Have you been fighting again?" He looked at Will, whose own coat was covered with Ink's blood.

The boy tried to pull away from his master, who held tightly to his collar.

Will didn't wait to see what the hooper would do. He lunged at the other boy, shouting, "Why did you do it?"

The apprentice barely had time to cover his face before Will's blow landed. Before Will could land another one, the hooper, who was a big man, grabbed him by the collar. He held the two boys at arms' length.

"What's going on here? Who are you?"

"My name's Will Northaway. I'm Mr. Spelman's boy."

"Ah, the Tory printer." A look of distaste crossed the hooper's face.

Will set his jaw. "Your boy killed my dog."

"That's quite a serious charge. Can you back it up?"

Will told his story, pulling the bloody rock out of his pocket and showing it to the man. When he had finished, the man turned to his apprentice, who was staring at the ground. Around them the snow fell steadily.

"Is this true?"

"I didn't do it," the boy said, refusing to look at Will.

His master twisted his collar. "Tell the truth!"

"I didn't do it," the boy whined. "It was Luke. We followed Spelman's lad, hoping to have a bit of fun with him. But Luke had to use his slingshot . . ."

Will's fists clenched and unclenched at his side. "I don't

believe him. He's been threatening me since we came, and now he's killed my dog."

The hooper released Will. "Go home, lad. Leave this boy to me. He'll pay for his part of it." The hooper turned and, without letting go of his apprentice, dragged him down the street.

TWELVE

Will blamed those boys for his dog's death. But the real blame, he thought, belonged to his master. If the man had not spoken out in defense of the king, all would be well. Ink would still be alive.

Bitterness ate away at the boy, and he went about his work grimly. The once-comfortable evenings in front of the fire reading the Bible had ended. Will sat and listened, but he hardened his heart against the words and against his master.

Perhaps if Mr. Spelman had not been so worried about his need for money, he would have paid more attention to his apprentice. As it was, he didn't notice the change in Will.

Christmas came and went with little celebration. Will continued to hunt for game, but it was lonely without Ink. Hunger made him press on.

Meanwhile, his master began meeting with Mr. Chandler. "I'm selling some of my books," the printer explained.

Will welcomed the coins that appeared after those visits, but he worried that the townspeople would take note of the meetings. "They'll think you're plotting against them," he warned his master.

"Ridiculous. They know my press has been shut down all winter. They can't blame me for trying to make ends meet."

Will didn't say any more, but his resentment against his master increased.

One particularly cold day, when gusty winds blew through the cracks in the sills and around the doors, Mr. Spelman rose from his chair in front of the fire and put his hand to his head. "I'm not feeling well. I'm going to bed."

Will watched his master shuffle up the stairs like an old man, his once-strong body nearly bent in half. A half hour later when Will went to look in on him, he found him burning with fever. A dry cough rattled in his chest.

The boy did not know what to do. Without a doctor, his master could die. Yet he had no way of paying for one. Will didn't even know whom to ask for help. He took the blanket off his own bed and covered his master with it. Then, pulling up a chair, he waited, uncertain what to do next.

Just sitting there nearly drove Will crazy. He watched his master toss and turn and felt powerless to help. Finally, able to stand it no longer, he decided to seek help from Mr. Chandler.

Will stepped out into the bitter cold and set out on the long walk to Mr. Chandler's farm on the outskirts of Worcester. On snowshoes he took off across the fields; a knife-sharp pain cut him as he looked down to where Ink should have been.

Will squinted against the sun, which reflected off the broad expanse of snow. With every breath his lungs burned, and his nose dripped onto his scarf. Still he hurried on.

When Will finally reached the farm, two barking hounds announced his presence. The door swung open before Will could knock, and a woman in an apron greeted him.

"Is Mr. Chandler in?" Will asked. The woman beckoned the boy to come in and pulled the door shut behind him.

"What is your business with my master?" she asked.

"I believe he is a friend of my master," the boy began.

"I mean . . ." He blushed and grew confused under her steady gaze.

She smiled and took pity on him. "You look cold. Let's go into the kitchen, and you can tell me what brings you out on such a bitter day."

Will followed her down highly polished halls into a kitchen with a large brick fireplace. She pointed at a wooden chair near the fire as she bustled around with the kettle. While she fixed tea, the boy began to thaw.

She handed him a cup of sweet, creamy tea and waited as he took a sip. Then she said, "Now tell me about your master."

"It's Mr. Spelman. He's taken very sick, and I'm afraid he may die if I don't get a doctor."

"Did you call on the apothecary? Surely you know that Mr. Chandler is not a doctor."

"But we have no money, and I don't know where to go."

"I see . . ."

Will took another sip of tea, letting the hot brew warm him while he waited for the woman to answer.

"Wait here, and I will see."

She disappeared through the door, and he looked around at the cozy kitchen where dried onions, herbs, and flowers hung from the beams. Freshly baked bread sat on the counter next to a pie. A turkey roasted in the fire. The tempting smells made him long to stay.

"My master is sending one of the maids, who is gifted in healing, to help. They are hooking up the sleigh now, and so you should come."

She led Will through the kitchen toward a door that opened into the back. Across a garden stood the stable, and Will could see several men hooking up the horses to a black-painted sleigh.

"Wait one minute," the woman instructed and ducked back inside. She returned with several hot bricks wrapped in towels. "These will keep your feet warm as you travel."

Will thanked her and climbed into the sleigh. A thin girl in a heavy coat sat next to him.

"What is your name?" the older woman asked as she loaded a basket into the back of the sleigh.

"Will Northaway . . . and thank you."

"Don't thank me; thank my master." Then pointing at the girl in the sleigh, she said, "This is Harmony. She'll care for your master. The driver will wait at the tavern for her." To Harmony she said, "You take care, child. God be with you."

Harmony smiled shyly at the older woman and clutched her coat tightly about her thin shoulders, and then they were off.

Will had never before been in a sleigh, and he enjoyed skimming over the frozen ground. The horses kept a steady pace, and they reached town all too soon.

Once he had shown Harmony his master's room, she busied herself with his care. Will stood around uselessly in the doorway until she had pity on him and gave him a task to do. "Boil some water, please."

Later that evening Harmony came downstairs with her basket. "He should rest well tonight. I've put a poultice on his chest for the cough and given him something for fever. You must make sure he drinks a bit more of this before he sleeps, and I'll be back tomorrow."

Will nodded.

"Come. Mrs. Harris sent food for your supper. There's a bit of meat and some bread and pie. You must eat and ward off sickness yourself. It will do your master no good for you to grow thin with worry."

Will's mouth watered as he smelled the food that she

brought forth from her basket. He began to offer her some, but she refused with a smile. "I'll have plenty at home."

She didn't wait for him to eat. Instead she darted across the snowy road to the tavern where the sleigh waited. Will took his meal upstairs and ate it while he watched his master sleep.

The fever lasted more than a week. Harmony came each morning and stayed for an hour or so. Each day she brought a basket with food for Mr. Spelman and something for Will as well.

When the printer had recovered, Harmony stopped coming. Will was glad that his master was better, but he missed the meals.

"Don't worry, lad," his master said. "Mr. Chandler and I have worked out an arrangement. I can pay him back for all this care and make a bit of money."

"Doing what?" the boy asked suspiciously.

"Printing a small broadside that he and Mr. Paine have written."

"But you can't publish," Will protested. "What about the tax?"

"I won't print on unstamped paper. That would be breaking the law, but Mr. Chandler is willing to pay for stamped paper."

Will shook his head. "I thought your illness might bring you to your senses," he grumbled. "It doesn't matter if what you do is legal. Is it right? All your neighbors can't be wrong when they argue that it's unjust for the king to pass taxes on us when we have no representatives in Parliament. It isn't fair."

"It isn't a question of fairness. There's one thing more important, and that is duty. If the Bible says we must obey those in authority over us, then we must do so—even when it hurts our own pocketbooks."

Will set his jaw and shook his head.

"You may not like it, son, but that's the way it is. Besides, I must make a living. I cannot continue like this. God's provision for me is this press. I must use it . . . or sell it."

"Would you do that?" Will had never imagined that his master might sell the press.

"I've thought about it. There hasn't been much else to think about this long winter. Even if I'm able to do a bit of work for Mr. Chandler, it's not enough to live on. I've thought about selling it and moving to England."

"England? Why?" Will looked horrified.

"If it becomes impossible for me to work at my trade, then I may not have a choice."

"I won't go." Will crossed his arms and glared at his master.

Mr. Spelman's face hardened. "Don't forget your place, Will Northaway. You may not want to go, but if I go, you'll go with me."

"It would be a stupid idea," the boy insisted.

"We won't talk of it now, but come spring, I may not have a choice. Right now Mr. Chandler will pay me for printing his broadside. I need the money, and I agree with what he says. Why should I refuse to print it?"

Will couldn't find an answer. But he was not happy; he knew once the townsmen discovered these broadsides, they would find a way of showing their anger.

THIRTEEN

In one way it felt good to have the press running again. Will was happy to do the familiar tasks and glad to see his master hunched over his composing table. When they had finished the first pages and hung them on the line to dry, Will and his master leaned back with satisfaction.

"I've missed it," Will admitted.

"Me too."

"If you sold the press, what would you do?"

"Perhaps buy another one in England. It's the only trade I know, though I suppose I could sell books. . . . But let's not waste time thinking about what might be. We have work to do here."

When the job was done and the pages dry, Mr. Spelman wrapped them in brown paper and tied the bundle carefully with twine. "I'd take them myself," he said to the boy, "but I'm not strong enough yet to brave the cold."

Will carried the papers to Mr. Chandler, and in return he brought home a purse filled with coins. It was the first of many visits to the farm, and after a while the boy no longer thought much about it. He didn't know what the squire did with the broadsides. He never saw them in town, but that wasn't his worry.

He and Mr. Spelman had also returned to their comfortable ways. After watching the hooper and other masters, Will was happy to have a master who treated him with kindness and patience. He often felt as though he was a son rather than an apprentice, especially when his master called him "son."

Still, in the back of his mind, Will knew that his master was engaged in a dangerous business. It was only a matter of time before someone realized that he was printing broadsides on stamped paper. And when the townsmen realized it, they would take action.

As spring came, it brought out mischief-makers. After having been housebound during the winter, they were looking for trouble. Stories of the latest pranks and petty crimes circulated through town. Fences had been cut at one farm, a chicken had been stolen from another, and several drunken youths had spent a night tipping over outhouses.

According to the king, all legal papers had to be written on stamped paper. Local courts, however, refused to use stamped paper; so the legal system shut down, and the young troublemakers, knowing they were out of reach of the law, continued to cause trouble.

Mr. Spelman heard the stories and nodded. "You see, Will," he said, "lawlessness brings more lawlessness. The judge set himself up against the king, and now these youths won't honor him."

One day the printer and Will left the door to the shop unlocked while working in the backyard. A half hour later they discovered that someone had come inside and knocked over cases of type, scattering them across the wooden floor.

Mr. Spelman stared at the mess. Though he rarely lost his temper since taking up Bible reading, he was furious. "Thugs, hooligans, scoundrels!" he shouted. "Get the constable, for I will pursue justice."

"But he won't be able to do anything," Will protested. "A legal writ must be on stamped paper, and the court won't use it."

Mr. Spelman paced back and forth. "They talk about tyranny from the king. What about the tyranny from the mob?"

Will worried that his master might have a fit, for his face had turned red, and a vein throbbed at his temple. "I'll pick up," he offered. "Perhaps nothing is missing, and no harm has been done." To make the point, he knelt down and began picking up and sorting the type.

"See," he said when he had picked up the mess, "it's all here. Someone was just having a bit of fun with us. No harm done." Although the boy spoke calmly, he was afraid. Clearly it was another warning.

Mr. Spelman sat down heavily and held his head between his hands. "Perhaps I will have to sell the press. They mean to destroy me."

Will pretended not to hear. He hoped that he could soothe his master's feelings and change his mind about selling. And he hoped the trouble would soon pass over.

Despite Will's protests, Mr. Spelman insisted on reporting the crime to the sheriff.

"There's not much I can do, sir," the sheriff said. "The courts are not pursuing any cases. If you suffered no loss, you should be thankful."

"But a crime—," Spelman began.

The sheriff interrupted. "Many in Worcester don't appreciate your activities," he said. "We value loyalty, and yet your loyalty to the king threatens all of us. I urge you to be careful."

"Is that a threat?" the printer demanded.

"Not a threat," the sheriff said. "But a warning. I can't be responsible for any trouble that you bring on yourself."

Mr. Spelman stormed out of the town hall. "Lawbreakers," he muttered under his breath. "All of them."

When he arrived back at the print shop, he began slapping type into boxes.

"What are you doing?" Will asked.

"Packing."

"For where?"

"Back to Boston. I'll sell the press, and we'll leave for England on the next ship."

Will was stunned. "But you said you'd never run. Besides, what will Mr. Chandler say? Don't you still owe him money?"

The printer's eyes narrowed as he mulled over the boy's words. He had promised to print four broadsides for the squire and had only finished three. "You're right. I will delay my departure to do the squire's work. But you must face it. We cannot stay."

Will was confused and fretted over his master's threat. He loved Mr. Spelman and wanted to follow him, but he hated London and what had happened to him there. He respected his master's views, but he also respected Sam Adams and Paul Revere. He feared the mobs in Boston, but he also feared the redcoats. How could good people so disagree? Why did Mr. Spelman believe his duty lay with the king when Sam Adams, also a religious man, believed his lay with liberty? Will couldn't understand.

He kept those thoughts to himself as he and his master worked alongside each other each day. By unspoken agreement they did not talk about the future.

Then one day Mr. Spelman summoned Will. "You must run an errand for me. Take this bottle to the tavern and have it filled with ale. While you are there, you will see Mr. Chandler, who has something for you."

"Why at the tavern?"

"Because he has noted odd fellows standing around near his gates, watching who comes and goes. It's much better that we meet in the open, for no one will think anything of it."

Will pulled on his hat and grabbed the bottle. "I'll be back soon," he promised.

Grass peeked through the melted snow, and water dripped from icicles. Buds swelled on the tips of tree branches, and birds filled the air with song.

Will hummed to himself as he crossed the Green to the tavern. Wagons filled the streets, and the tavern was crowded with men who had come to town for seed and other necessities. He waited for the keeper to notice him. While he stood waiting, he saw Mr. Chandler huddled over a table with Mr. Paine. He paid them no mind, because he wasn't supposed to draw attention to himself.

The tavern keeper appeared. "How can I help you, lad?"

"My master asks you to fill this with ale," Will said. The boy felt nervous, as though every eye in the tavern was on him. He studied the floor while he waited for the man to fill his bottle from one of the barrels. As Mr. Chandler rose from his seat and walked toward him, Will heard the door behind him slam. He turned and caught a glimpse of a boy staring at him through the window. *I'm just being jumpy*, he thought.

Mr. Chandler interrupted his thoughts. "How is Mr. Spelman?" he asked.

"Much better, thank you," Will answered.

As they spoke, Mr. Chandler slipped a piece of paper into the boy's pocket and then put on his hat as he opened the door.

"Tell him I hope the Lord prospers him and his business," he said.

"Yes, sir."

The tavern keeper finished filling the bottle and handed it back. Will paid him and headed out the door. He looked up the street and saw Mr. Chandler entering the apothecary.

When he looked the other way, he caught sight of someone darting around a corner. He laughed nervously. "Samuel would tell me I'm acting like a girl," he chided himself. "There's no one there." He shook off his nervousness and turned in the direction of home. But the day was so beautiful that Will couldn't bear to return to the shop quite yet. He wished he had brought the musket, but even without it, a walk would be pleasant.

He glanced toward the print shop and hesitated. "It won't hurt if I take the long way home," he muttered.

The long way meant going out of town, cutting though the woods, and circling back through the fields. It would give Will a chance to pass the beaver pond and see if the ice had melted. He whistled as he walked, and the music calmed him. Twice he heard sounds behind him, but when he whirled around, he saw nothing.

A skim of ice still covered the surface of the pond, trapping air bubbles underneath it. Thin cracks zigzagged across the surface. Will found some rocks and lobbed them at the ice. The small ones skittered across, but when he threw a large one, the ice shuddered and cracked apart, sending the rock to the pond bottom.

Will heard a noise and looked up, but he saw nothing but clumps of snow dropping from the trees to the ground. He reached his hand into his pocket and felt the note that Mr. Chandler had given him. He looked around nervously before pulling it out and staring at it. Since it was sealed with wax, he couldn't open it. He shoved it back into his pocket.

He suddenly wished he was home. The deep silence of the woods pressed down on him. Every noise startled him, and the presence of the secret letter in his pocket made him feel afraid. "All this mischief is making me nervous," he told himself, but, nonetheless, he bent and picked up his bottle, determined to head home.

He had just straightened up when he heard a footfall. He looked around and saw the hooper's apprentice, axe in hand, blocking his way.

"Are you following me?" Will asked more boldly than he felt.

"Ever since the tavern," the apprentice answered. "Give me what's in your pocket."

"I don't know what you're talking about," Will said, backing away. As he turned to run, however, he found his way blocked by two other boys.

"What're you doing?"

"We want to know what's in your pocket."

"I told you already. I don't have anything." Will's hand slipped unconsciously into his pocket, where he fingered the letter. He eyed the boys, who began inching toward him. "Which one of you killed my dog?" he demanded.

"The judge said it was an accident," one of the boys answered.

"I know it was no accident," Will said, clenching his fists.

"Grab him," the hooper's boy yelled.

Will saw him lunge, and from the corner of his eye he saw the other boys dart toward him. Before any of them could reach him, he darted off the path through the trees. Will was a fast runner, but the ground was slick, and trees slowed him down. Heavy footsteps pursued him, pushing him to run faster and faster.

When the forest finally thinned, Will hoped to catch sight of town. Instead he found himself on the edge of a corn-field. He slipped and slid through the muddy field. Behind him a boy cursed as he tripped. Resisting the urge to turn around and see how much distance he'd gained, Will kept running.

Ahead a faint wisp of smoke drifted into the sky, and then a rooftop and chimney lurched into view. With relief he ran into a farmyard, bending over and gasping for air. Warily he watched as his pursuers slowed down. "You'll have to get me another time," he taunted from the safety of the farmyard.

"Grab him, George."

Will couldn't believe it. The boys didn't stop. Before he realized that they still meant to do him harm, the one named George had thrown him to the ground. The other two boys were quick to pile on. "What're you doing?" Will spat mud from his mouth.

"You picked the wrong farm," the hooper's boy laughed. His name was Amos, and he seemed to be the leader. "This is George's place, and his father is gone. We would have brought you here if you hadn't done the job yourself."

Will squirmed, but one of the boys twisted his arm behind him. "Give us the letter."

Will tried to twist away, but they jerked his arm so violently that he cried out in pain.

"Hand it over," George demanded. When Will refused, they rolled him over, and while two of them held him still, the other searched his pocket.

"Here it is. I've got it."

"You probably can't even read," Will managed to say before Amos cuffed him across the face. George blushed at the boy's taunt and shoved the paper at Amos.

"You read it."

Amos broke the seal and pulled the heavy paper out of the envelope. "It's a letter to the governor, naming all the men in Worcester who are against the king."

"What was your master going to do with this?"

Will was as surprised as the other boys about the content of the letter. He didn't know what his master had wanted to do with it; so he shrugged and said nothing.

Amos slapped him again. "I don't know anything," Will protested. "You should ask him."

Amos stood up. "Drag him to the fire," he ordered. By now Will could smell the sharp odor of hot tar, which was familiar from his time at sea. He struggled to free himself, but the three boys tightened their grip.

"I think he smells the tar," Amos said.

A small bonfire burned in the middle of the yard. Over it hung an iron kettle.

Amos grabbed Will's ankle and pulled him across the muddy yard. When Will struggled to free himself, George kicked him in the ribs.

"Hold him tight."

"Watch him squirm."

As they laughed and taunted Will, George stirred the pot. "He'll learn where his loyalties lie," he laughed.

Will groaned as they spread steaming black tar onto his coat. Some splattered on his neck and face. He howled with pain, but that only seemed to spur on his attackers. They kicked him again as they poured more tar onto his body. Amos then picked up a pail of turkey feathers and dumped them over him.

Will lay still, hoping they'd go away.

"Do you think we killed him?" George looked frightened. "My dad will have my hide."

"He's not dead. Look . . ." Amos kicked Will again until he groaned. "See, he's fine. He's just too scared to get up."

"I'm getting out of here," one of the boys said.

"Me too," George added. "Remember, Amos, it was your idea."

"You're cowards," Amos sneered. "Run away. I don't care."

Will listened to the sound of footsteps fading away. When he opened his eyes, Amos was standing over him.

"Get up," the hooper's boy demanded.

"I can't," Will whimpered. "You broke my ribs."

"Get up." Amos angrily grabbed Will's arm and pulled him to his feet. "Take this warning to your master."

"You won't get away with this," Will groaned.

"I wouldn't be sure of that. Now run home and give Spelman our warning."

The hardened tar made it almost impossible for the boy to walk. He had lost his bottle somewhere, and now he'd lost the letter. He wanted to escape into a hole and die, but he was in too much pain.

After nearly two hours he staggered through the door and fell at his master's feet. "What happened to you?" Mr. Spelman roared. "Who did this?"

Will shook his head. "It doesn't matter. They'll never be punished, and if we cause them trouble, they'll just do it again."

Try as he might, Mr. Spelman could not get the boy to talk. Finally, he gave up and worked at removing the tar-soaked clothes, being careful not to touch the tar on Will's face and neck.

"Does it hurt?" he asked as he cut through the cloth.

"My chin feels like it's on fire," the boy groaned.

Mr. Spelman scowled. "What kind of cowards are they to punish a boy for the ideas of the master?" As he cut away the coat, tears rolled down his cheek. Then he wrapped the boy in a soft blanket and left him in front of the fire.

"I don't know how to remove that tar," he said. "I'm afraid if I pull, it will tear away your skin. Try to sleep. I'm going for help."

When Will woke, he found gentle Harmony leaning over him, dabbing fragrant oil on the tar and gently peeling the black sticky stuff away. He gritted his teeth as she worked, determined not to yell. When she was done, she applied ointment and loosely wrapped his wounds.

"Though it burn, sweet Will, you must not pull or scratch. It is blistered and will grow infected if you do. I will give your master this lotion to soothe your wounds."

Will smiled wanly. "Thank you," he whispered.

"I'm sorry," she said. "Though bad men did this to you, don't hold it against all of us. There are many good people in Worcester."

Will nodded. "I know, though my master no longer believes that."

When Will next awoke, he found his master kneeling on the floor next to the bed. Before Will drifted once more into sleep, he heard Mr. Spelman say, "Lord, have mercy. What have I done?"

FOURTEEN

Word of Will's tarring and feathering quickly spread through Worcester. A stream of visitors trickled by the shop, some to sympathize, some to gawk, and some to apologize for the actions of a few. Though Mr. Spelman was polite to them, Will sensed his anger in the stubborn set of his shoulders.

When the judge came, Will pretended to sleep.

"You must wake the boy so we can discover who did this."

"He won't talk to you," Mr. Spelman said, shaking his head. "Though you threaten him, he'll keep his silence."

"Why is he so stubborn?"

"Because he says you'll do nothing. Without stamped paper there can be no writ, and you won't accept stamped paper."

"Aye, he's right. We won't give the king the satisfaction. But perhaps we could punish the boys another way."

"Then you would be as lawless as they," said the printer.

Finally, the judge left, and Will rolled over and stared at his master, who slumped in his chair, holding his head heavily in his hands. After a time he rose up, closed the shutters, and latched the door. As he walked back toward the fire, he noticed the boy watching him.

"How long have you been awake?"

"Long enough to hear the judge."

"You should tell what you know."

"It'll make no difference," Will repeated wearily.

"I know who I blame," Mr. Spelman declared. "Boys may have done it, but the Sons of Liberty are behind it."

"They had nothing to do with it," the boy cried.

"Will Northaway, are you foolish enough to think that boys care a bit about taxes or rights? The only ideas in their fool heads were put there by the fine Sons of Liberty."

"But the Sons of Liberty are against violence," Will protested.

"Just words. In my eyes they are as guilty as the ones who slung the tar."

"I tried to warn you," Will said.

"Do you think I've not been thinking about that? I never intended to put you at risk, and I'm sorrier than you can imagine for what happened."

Neither Will nor his master brought up the subject of moving, though it was clearly on both their minds. They were more careful. Will rarely ventured out alone. When he did, he felt as though he was an object of pity, curiosity, or hostility. He felt as though some people blamed him for causing trouble.

The next few weeks were filled with rumors. Riders from Boston hinted that the king had canceled the Stamp Tax. But there were other rumors of higher taxes and new penalties. Finally, word came that the king had backed down. The Sons of Liberty rejoiced, but Mr. Spelman fell into a black mood, convinced that the king's show of weakness would lead to greater violence in the future.

The king's action made the patriots bolder. Normally cautious merchants now spoke freely about independence. Instead of love between the king and his subjects, anger grew.

Newspapers brought stories from New York where the king insisted that soldiers be housed in the homes of ordinary people. The colonists hated it and refused to let the redcoats in. Mr. Spelman grew more and more withdrawn.

Now that the Stamp Tax had ended, the printer expected business to improve. But it did not. Will knew the problem: The people of Worcester didn't trust them. They were seen as loyal to the king, and the people no longer wanted to serve the king; so they took their business elsewhere.

One beautiful spring day, Mr. Spelman threw open the shutters and propped open the door. A lilac-scented breeze blew through the shop, tugging at paper and wafting away the stale smell of wood smoke.

"I've made up my mind," he said, standing at the door with his hands on his hips.

"What do you mean?" Will asked.

"I've sold the press to a man in Boston. He'll pay me a fair price for it."

Will held his breath, fearing what would come next.

"I'm going to England." The printer turned and looked at the boy.

Will stared at the floor, saying nothing.

"I know you don't want to go back. I can't blame you . . ." The words seemed difficult for Mr. Spelman to say.

Will waited.

"So I've sold your papers to Mr. Mein along with the press. You'll stay in Boston." The printer took a deep breath.

Will sank into a chair. He had not imagined a future without Mr. Spelman, who had become like a father to him. "But I thought . . . I thought I could convince you to stay." Will barely got the words out.

"I can't stay. I don't even want to. This place no longer feels like my home. Everything I've come to believe tells me that my duty lies with the king. I wish it could be otherwise, but it isn't." The printer sighed deeply and moved about restlessly.

"But what about me?"

"I've written to Mein. He seems to be a good man. He sells books and wants to start a newspaper. His credit is good, and I hear nothing bad of him. He has promised to treat you well and continue your training. He's a pious man, from all accounts."

"It's settled then?"

"Yes, son."

"Don't call me that," Will shouted. "I'm not your son—just your property."

FIFTEEN

Three weeks later, after an easy journey, Will and Mr. Spelman were once again in Boston, walking down familiar streets, smelling the salt air, and eating Mrs. Simpson's food. The printer's trunks were packed for the trip to England, and he waited only for Will's old ship, the *Ana Eliza*, to arrive.

On the second day back Will and his master walked to Mr. Mein's shop, squeezed between a blacksmith and a tanner on an out-of-the way street in Boston's old North End. The street stank, and Will wrinkled his nose.

"Smells like London," he complained.

"Shh. Stop complaining."

Will looked sideways at his master, whose face had aged in the past year. "It'll be strange . . ."

"For both of us." Mr. Spelman stopped in front of the shop and stared through the dusty window. The walls were lined with book-filled shelves.

"It's small," Will whispered.

"Big enough for the press and a table," Mr. Spelman answered.

He pushed open the door, and a thin man with graying red hair looked up from a small desk. Before he could speak, Mr. Spelman strode forward with his hand out. "Are you John Mein? I'm William Spelman. We've been corresponding about my press."

The red-haired man stood up. He was a short, rail-thin fellow who wore wire-rimmed spectacles at the end of his nose. "Welcome, welcome. Did you have a good trip back?"

"The Lord prospered it," Mr. Spelman answered. Then looking down at Will, who stood nervously at his side, he said, "This is my lad, Will Northaway."

Mr. Mein studied the boy as though he was a horse or a cow for sale. Will blushed under his gaze. "We'll have time to get acquainted later, Will Northaway. If you're a hard worker, honest, and obedient, we'll get on well." With a nod of his head he dismissed him and turned his attention back to Mr. Spelman.

The two men were a study in contrasts. Though Mr. Spelman had lost weight in Worcester, he was still a stocky man with a large neck and big, square hands. Mr. Mein was about the same height, but his thinness made him appear much smaller. His voice was soft (Will had to lean forward to hear it), while Mr. Spelman tended to bellow, even when he was happy. The boy watched as they agreed on a time to deliver the press and sign papers. As they talked, he began to feel more anxious.

When he and his master left the shop, Will lashed out at Mr. Spelman. "I don't like him. Why must I work for him? It isn't fair."

Mr. Spelman stopped in the middle of the street and grabbed Will's shoulder. "Listen to me, Will Northaway. God has brought us to this place. I can't stay here; you don't want to go back to England. I understand that. If you want to come with me, say so, and I will tell Mr. Mein. But if not . . ."

Will's eyes filled with tears. "I hate you," he snarled, pulling his arm away and running down the street.

Mr. Spelman watched him run, praying that he'd find a way to comfort the boy.

As they waited for the *Ana Eliza* to arrive, Will avoided

his master. It wasn't hard to do because Mr. Spelman spent his days at Mein's shop, showing him the fine points of the press, or at the taverns catching up on the local news.

Will spent his days with Samuel, who had grown up over the past year. His friend was tall and strong. Samuel's mother had finally agreed, after months of his nagging, that he could go to sea. He too waited eagerly for the *Ana Eliza* to arrive.

Only Will seemed to dread the ship's arrival. When it came, his life would change forever.

Every morning Samuel scanned the horizon for the three-masted ship. When he'd turn away with disappointment, Will's spirits would rise. But one morning at the beginning of June, Will woke to Samuel's excited shouts. "It's here! I swear it is. Three masts. Look at them!"

Will jumped up and pressed his face to the small attic window. His heart lurched when he saw the ship. Though it looked like the *Ana Eliza*, he urged caution. "There are lots of three-masted ships. It may not be her."

They hurriedly dressed and rushed downstairs, waving away Mrs. Simpson's pleas that they eat something first. "Later, Mother," Samuel said. "The ship is here."

Her smile faded, and the light in her eyes dimmed. She turned away, but not fast enough to keep Will from seeing her tears.

"Your mother doesn't want you to leave," he said to his friend as they turned into the street.

"Why do you say that?"

"Did you see her face? She's sad that the ship has come. Don't you feel bad about leaving?"

"I can't stay here. I'm grown up, and I need to make my way in the world."

Will shook his head but said nothing. How strange it

was, he thought, that he should long for a father and be twice disappointed while Samuel, who had a mother, would easily give her up.

They reached the dock, and the *Ana Eliza* came into full view. "She's beautiful," Samuel sighed.

"She is at that," Will agreed. Now that he saw the ship, he felt nervous and excited about seeing the old crew. "Do you think Mr. Mattison is aboard?"

"Of course he is. In fact, he's captain now. Didn't you know?"

"When did that happen?"

"Old Captain Boyd became sick, and he sold his stake to Mr. Mattison."

Will paused on the dock and stared at his friend. "He'll be a good captain. Don't think he'll go easy on you."

"He's already told me that he'll work me to death. I believe him. Said if I didn't want to work, I should sign on with another captain." Samuel grinned as he talked, happy as he thought about his future at sea.

As the boys watched the ship, they heard a voice behind them. "Samuel Simpson?"

Will and Samuel turned to see Captain Mattison striding down the dock, his ditty bag slung over his shoulder. Samuel ran towards the captain and threw his arms around him. Then embarrassed, he stood back and grinned at the tall, bronzed man.

"You remember Will Northaway, don't you?" Samuel pointed at Will.

"Aye! How are you? You've become a young man." He slapped Will on the back approvingly and threw his arms over their shoulders. "Lead me home. I'm dying for some good cooking. Has your beautiful mother found a husband yet?"

Samuel laughed. "She's too busy worrying about me."

When they reached the house, Mrs. Simpson was pulling hot griddle cakes out of the fire. "John," she said, wiping her eyes with the corner of her apron. "How good it is to see you. How was your trip?"

"Couldn't have been better."

"You must be hungry. There's plenty. Sit, sit . . ." She brought a platter of sliced ham and a bowl of stewed fruit to the table. Then she stood nearby, refilling his plate as soon as it was empty. Finally, he looked up from his plate and smiled at her.

"Sit down, Deborah. You're making me nervous, for I'm not used to all this attention."

"I doubt that, Captain Mattison," she said fondly. "Did the men take to your leadership?"

"We had a few rough patches, a bit of testing, but nothing I didn't expect. It's a good crew. Samuel will learn a great deal from them."

Again Mrs. Simpson's face fell. Her bottom lip trembled. Captain Mattison reached out and patted her hand. "It'll be fine. I'll take good care of him. You need not fear."

She smiled weakly. "I know I'm being silly," she admitted. "But it's hard to let him go."

"Oh, Ma," Samuel said, "you promised you wouldn't get all weepy."

As they were finishing breakfast, Mr. Spelman walked in. "John!" He shook the sailor's hand. "Good to see you."

"I thought you were in Worcester."

"I was, but it's a long tale. Do you have room to take me back with you?"

"Visiting England?"

"Moving there, I'm afraid."

Captain Mattison stared at the others around the table. "What's going on?"

Will shrugged. Mrs. Simpson shook her head. "We live in strange times," she replied. "My brother no longer feels loyalty to the colonies; so he goes back to England."

Mr. Mattison looked stunned. "Will you go with him?"

Mrs. Simpson shook her head. "I will miss him, but my home is here. My loyalties are here. My memories are here." As she spoke, her eyes welled with tears.

Mr. Spelman smiled at his sister before turning to the captain. "If you'll take me," he said, "I'll have plenty of time to tell you my stories. Will you?"

"I'd be honored to have you aboard. We'll set sail in two weeks."

"Two weeks!" Samuel and Will spoke at the same time. For the one it seemed an eternity, and for the other it seemed much too short.

But finally the day came. Captain Mattison was already aboard, overseeing last-minute preparations. Samuel carried his trunk to the pier and watched as two sailors loaded it onto a dinghy. He turned and faced his mother and Will, who had come to see the ship off. She looked very small and lonely among the sailors. Will stood protectively at her side.

"Be good," she whispered. "God protect you."

Samuel gave her a quick hug before climbing into the boat. Then Mr. Spelman cleared his throat. "No speeches," he promised.

"I'm scared," Will whispered.

"I am too. But remember one thing, lad—whatever happens, you aren't alone. There is a great God who rules over all things, even the lives of printer's devils in Boston. Put your trust in him, and you need not be afraid."

Will nodded, not sure that he understood, but he felt comforted by his master's words.

The printer followed Samuel into the boat. Two sailors took up their oars and began to row. Slowly the boat cut its way toward the ship.

"Good-bye," they called after it.

"May God be with you, lad," Mr. Spelman yelled.

"And with you," the boy whispered. Then he and Mrs. Simpson turned and walked home.